Ben's disarming grin weakened her already shaky defenses.

"Well—perhaps—maybe sometime," she conceded.

"That's what my mother used to say when she meant no." The grin widened. "So, is that no maybe or yes maybe?"

Tassy couldn't help the little smile. "That's just maybe, Ben."

"Definitely maybe?"

She felt a little hiccup in the region of her heart. "Definitely maybe," she said firmly, and wondered why it felt as if she'd said yes.

"Progress, then," he said, his lips twitching. "We've gone from definitely no to definitely maybe. Things are looking up."

Caroline Anderson's nursing career was brought to an abrupt halt by a back injury, but her interest in medical things led her to work first as a medical secretary, and then, after completing her teacher training, as a lecturer in medical office practice to trainee medical secretaries. She lives in rural Suffolk with her husband, two daughters and assorted animals.

Prescription: Romance™

DEFINITELY
MAYBE
CAROLINE ANDERSON

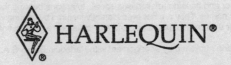

TORONTO · NEW YORK · LONDON
AMSTERDAM · PARIS · SYDNEY · HAMBURG
STOCKHOLM · ATHENS · TOKYO · MILAN · MADRID
PRAGUE · WARSAW · BUDAPEST · AUCKLAND

ISBN 0-373-83382-2

DEFINITELY MAYBE

First North American Publication 1998.

Copyright © 1998 by Caroline Anderson.

CHAPTER ONE

TASSY stared.

It was one of those things. One minute she was quietly minding her own business and getting on with her work, and the next minute there he was almost under her nose, the most gorgeous man she'd ever seen in her life, messing up her blood pressure with a vengeance.

Not that it mattered. Even if he marched right up to her and said she was the most wonderful thing he'd ever clapped eyes on it wouldn't make any difference because there was no way she was getting involved with anyone ever again.

Even if he did have floppy dark blond hair and aristocratic cheekbones and the most fantastic laughing jade-green eyes, and even if he was taller than her, remarkable though that was, with a body to die for. Apart from anything else, his taste in ties was deplorable. Who in their right mind would have shocking pink elephants dancing over their shirt front? His eyes, though, were gorgeous—

Damn. He was looking straight back at her, those gorgeous green eyes locked with hers, trapping her. She felt her heart skid and flutter, and slow heat crawled over her skin.

She turned back to the child she was feeding and coaxed one last teaspoonful of high-protein jelly into the reluctant mouth, dismissing the man. 'Well done,' she murmured, and then the hair on the back of her neck stood up on end and she hauled in a lungful of air and looked up—straight into those wonderful green eyes.

The fathers, she thought absently, got better-looking by the minute—and she was in serious danger of losing her professionalism. 'Is there anything I can do for you?' she asked, and was disgusted to hear that husky Mae West tone in her voice. Get a grip, girl, she told herself crossly.

'Sister Franklin?' he said with a lazy, sexy smile that sent her pulse rate soaring into the hereafter. So much for getting a grip! 'I'm Benedict Lazaar.'

'Lazaar—?' She groped about in her memory. There was no child by that name, but perhaps a stepfather?

'*Dr* Lazaar,' he added helpfully.

Oh, hell. The memory, she thought, was a defective organ on occasions. She smiled weakly. 'Of course. Sorry. It's been one of those days.'

He noticed her confusion, of course. If he'd been generous he would have ignored it, but of course he wasn't. His grin would have melted the polar icecaps. She straightened, dropped the spoon back into the jelly plate and stood up, scrubbing her slightly sticky hand down her uniform before holding it out to him. 'Pleased to meet you, Dr Lazaar. Welcome to the ward...'

She fizzled to a halt, conscious of the cool, strong fingers wrapped around the back of her hand, the warm, dry palm against hers, the sheer size of his hand engulfing hers. His thumb was against her pulse point—

She all but snatched her hand back and glanced at the child. 'We've finished here, haven't we, Sam? I'll just clear away our mess and I'll be with you, Dr Lazaar. Ask one of the nurses to show you into my office, would you?'

And she turned her back on him and fussed the eight-year-old in a way which she knew he would find highly tiresome while she struggled with her unexpected and thoroughly inconvenient response. Fancy letting her hormones get the better of her—at her age! Almost grinding her teeth with frustration, she smoothed Sam's hair back from his brow which earned her a dirty look, and then she left him in peace while she went to find the man who was going to be a thorn in her side.

How could she work with him? She couldn't look at him without her knees turning to slush. It was going to be tediously obvious that she found him attractive, even if her body was destined to be overruled by her mind. A man with looks like that was going to be altogether too aware of his effect on women, and, judging by that lazy grin, he was only too happy to act on their unbridled enthusiasm!

Oh, double damn, she thought, and, pushing open the door of her office, she found herself nose to nose with the object of her frustrations.

'I was just coming to look for you,' he told her with a grin.

That grin again.

And that stupid heart jiggling about again.

She sneaked in a surreptitious lungful of air and dredged up a smile. 'Well, I'm here. Want a cup of tea?'

'Have you got time?'

'I'll make time—I haven't had a break yet today and it's after two. I thought you weren't coming till tomorrow?'

She bustled about, plugging in the kettle and putting teabags in the mugs, hunting for biscuits—

'I wasn't. I'm not. I thought I'd just come and make

myself known, have a quick squint round the ward, flick through the notes—you know the sort of thing.'

She didn't, in fact, because nobody else ever did it. They arrived on the ward on their first morning, armed with white coats and stethoscopes if they were dead organised and a hangover from a farewell party if they weren't, and expected to be able to function usefully on the spot.

Maybe this one was different—and maybe pigs flew. Still, Josh had worked out all right, or so she'd heard. It was before her time, of course. The ward sister in those days had been Melissa Shaw, now Josh's wife and the mother of his two delectable children. Obviously she hadn't found him too irksome to work with!

Their new appointee was there because Josh had just become a junior consultant, a newly created post in an expanding department, and this man who was filling up her office and trampling all over her personal space with that to-die-for body was his replacement as Special Registrar for Andrew Barrett.

She wondered how he'd measure up to Josh, and thought he'd probably come up short on everything except stature—and maybe charm. That, like his sheer size, he seemed to have in abundance. The mothers, she thought crossly, would love him.

She handed him a cup of tea, perched on the edge of her chair and tried not to notice the neat hips propped against the windowsill just inches from her shoulder. He was blocking out half the light, and also—she wasn't sure if it was deliberate—making his face impossible to read with the light behind him.

She fiddled with her spoon, chasing bubbles round the

top of the cup, and asked him politely—to fill the silence—where he'd come from.

'London,' he told her, and shuddered eloquently.

She blinked. 'I take it you didn't like it,' she said drily, and he laughed.

'No. You either like it or you don't. As you say, I didn't. There are those who think it's a flaw in me.' His smile faded, leaving her with the distinct impression that there was more, much more, that he could have said.

He shifted, moving away from the window and prowling round her office, fiddling with the notices and prodding things curiously. She had a sudden vision of him in her home, doing the same thing—prowling through her personal possessions with that casual curiosity—and she had an almost overwhelming urge to smack his hand.

'The notes are there—in the trolley,' she told him, smacking down her cup instead so that the hardly touched contents slopped over into the saucer. 'Feel free to browse. I have to get on.'

And, pushing herself to her feet, she went out of the room and left him. As she did so her aura seemed to expand without the pressure of his presence to crowd it, and it felt as if she could breathe again...

Ben was twitchy. He hadn't felt twitchy for years, not like this. He couldn't sit still, his body suffused with a restless energy, his mind blanked out by the image of Sister Franklin branded on his brain. She was stunning—tall, strong yet slender, the supple curve of her spine as she'd bent over the child making him ache to draw her back against his chest and feel the healthy body align with his.

Her uniform wasn't the typical sister's uniform, but a

royal blue dress like the other nurses' white ones with a tabard top over it, brightly decorated with nursery characters. Even so, he could see the slim line of her waist and the subtle, womanly swell of her hips. Her hair was dark, touched with red, scraped up under a frilly hat out of the way. He wondered how long it was and how it would feel threaded between his fingers, and then he remembered the wary but curious look in those softest of brown eyes and wondered who had hurt her.

With a sigh he turned away from the window onto the ward and, sitting down where she had sat, pulled the trolley full of notes towards him, settled himself down and began to flick through them. Maybe they'd help to take his mind off her and make him concentrate on why he was here, and not just why he was going to like it...

Tassy went back to Sam. He was bored, uncomfortable and restless, and Tassy was worried about him. He had rheumatic fever, very rarely seen these days, and his heart was affected, as well as his joints in turn and his muscles. He was propped up in bed with cot sides because he had chorea, uncontrolled body movements which he hated, and they had to make sure he didn't fall out of bed.

It didn't seem to matter how many times Tassy promised him it was temporary, he was convinced it wasn't. He thought he would writhe and twitch indefinitely, he was often conscious of his irregular heartbeat and he was basically one very scared and unhappy little boy.

'Who's the dude with the tie?' Sam asked as she approached.

'Our new registrar. He'll be looking after you.'

'What about Dr Lancaster?'

'He's a consultant now. You'll still see him, but you're Dr Barrett's patient, really, and Dr Lazaar is working on Dr Barrett's team.'

'The tie's gross. I like Dr Lancaster better.'

Tassy grinned. 'I have to agree about the tie, but he's not really here today officially. I expect tomorrow's will be better.'

'Tomorrow's what?'

Sam and Tassy both jumped guiltily.

'Tie,' Sam said directly, while Tassy was casting about for a diplomatic lie.

Dr Lazaar picked up the tie dangling down his chest, looked at it and cocked an eyebrow. 'You don't like my tie? I thought it was a cool tie.'

Sam rolled his eyes, and Ben and the pink elephants lounged against the locker and mocked Tassy.

She rushed to fill the silence. 'I was just explaining that you were actually not working until tomorrow and that tomorrow's tie would probably be—quieter.'

'Quieter?'

'Mmm. You know...' Tassy flapped a hand and blushed a little. 'Less...'

'Loud?'

'Mmm.'

He grinned, quite unabashed. 'Sorry. This is one of my discreet ties.'

Tassy choked a little, and Sam groaned and rolled his eyes. 'Oh, man, a fashion freak,' he muttered. Dr Lazaar, to do him credit, just grinned again.

'Don't worry, it's my only vice,' he assured the boy, and then turned away. 'Well, almost,' he said *sotto voce* to Tassy in passing.

Tassy, her imagination leaping to life, blushed furiously and looked anywhere but into those damnable laughing green eyes...

'So, what can you tell me about Sister Franklin?'

Josh Lancaster's eyes tracked searchingly over Ben's face. Ben did his best to keep his expression neutral and innocent, but it was hard. The darned woman had fascinated him so much he'd hardly had any sleep, and that had been distinctly X-rated.

He'd been good, though. He'd asked about the ward, about the patients, about the routine and systems and methodology before he'd allowed himself to ask the one question he'd really wanted the answer to.

And now Josh was studying him thoughtfully. 'She's excellent. A real asset to the ward—why?'

'Just professional curiosity about a colleague.'

Josh twitched an eyebrow disbelievingly, and Ben gave a wry grin. 'I did happen to notice, as well, that she has—ah—rather long legs—'

'And a good body, and a most attractive face, and a lovely smile, and gorgeous hair, and the sweetest, kindest nature you could wish to find. She also has a sense of humour like a rapier, a very low opinion of men in general and flirts in particular, and she's definitely off limits.' His smile faded, his eyes suddenly serious. 'Sorry, buddy, you'll have to find yourself another toy. Tassy doesn't play.'

'Tassy?'

'Mmm. She's actually Natasha, but nobody dares to call her that. She loathes it.'

'Russian?'

'No, not Russian, English as the day is long. Her mother wanted her to be a ballerina.'

Ben filed that. Ballerinas were not his best thing at the moment. Still... His brows quirked. 'Married?'

'I believe she has been,' Josh said economically. 'She doesn't talk about it. I suggest you don't.'

'But it's put her off men.'

Josh nodded. ''Fraid so. Like I said, you'll have to find another playmate.'

Ben's face lost its smile. 'Who said I was looking for a playmate?'

Josh's eyes speared him like blue lasers. 'I don't know what you're looking for, Ben. Whatever it is, look elsewhere. Tassy definitely isn't interested in men.'

In men maybe not, Ben thought, but she'd been interested in him. He knew that, just as he knew that she didn't want to be and hated herself for it. She came into the room behind them and he felt his heart kick even before he turned round and saw her.

He hadn't felt like this for years, not since he was twenty or thereabouts. Sex didn't seem to have a great deal to do with it, either, although he couldn't deny his interest in that department. It just seemed to be so much more than that, a great surge of protectiveness brought about by the wounded look in her eyes and the wariness with which she avoided eye contact with him except when absolutely necessary.

And then, when it *was* necessary, when she couldn't avoid it, she stared almost defiantly into his eyes as if she were challenging him to dare to breach her defences.

Lord, he was tempted. Almost tempted enough to forget... He turned towards her now and found her looking at Josh.

'Sam's knee's sore,' she was saying. 'I think his poly-arthritis has found another site, and his leg keeps twitching and it's hurting him. Which one of you is going to deal with it?'

Josh looked at Ben and shrugged. 'Technically, he's yours. Want me to come too, just this time, or can you cope?'

Ben gave a wry grin. 'I think I can just about cope. What's his drug regimen?'

Josh pulled a set of notes out of the trolley and handed them to Ben. 'Steroids, because of the heart involvement. However, he's sensitive to them and we were considering taking him off them and putting him onto salicylates—soluble aspirin if we can get him to drink it. We'll need to taper off the steroids—I think you'll need to discuss it with Andrew. It might be that you'd want to sedate him to control the movements of his limbs until this bout of inflammation settles down. It's all on the chart.'

Ben nodded. 'OK. I'll go and have a chat to him. Think he'll approve of the tie?'

Tassy looked at it and a reluctant smile touched her eyes. 'I have my doubts, but it'll give him something else to think about.'

'Mmm. That's what I thought.' He patted the luminous green frogs with affection. 'Right, Sister Franklin, lead on.'

She led, horribly conscious of his large and very masculine frame so close behind her. He was wearing, in addition to the frogs, a lemon-yellow shirt that would have made anyone else look sick, forest green cords and desert boots. He moved almost silently—amazing for such a large man—and she felt distinctly as if she was being stalked.

Absurd. He was *supposed* to be following her.

She went into the little side room that held Sam, her eight-year-old patient with rheumatic fever, and grinned at him. 'It's Dr Lazaar to see you,' she told him. '*And his frogs!*' she added in a hiss.

Sam peered round her and rolled his eyes. 'Oh, yummy,' he said, deadpan.

'Glad you like it, son,' Ben said easily and, propping his big hands on the edge of the bed, he leant over and grinned. 'Now, what's this I hear about you feeling a bit rough? Leg hurting?'

Sam nodded. 'My left knee—no, my right—oh, I don't know. This one.'

He pointed to his left knee, and Ben folded back the bedclothes and studied it for a moment.

Good, Tassy thought, he's not touching it yet—just looking. That was always a good sign. He scanned the heart monitor briefly, then looked down at the knee again. 'Can you move it for me?' he asked gently.

Sam shook his head. 'It hurts when I move it, and it keeps twitching.'

As he said that the leg jerked involuntarily and Sam cried out, turning to Tassy and burrowing into her chest for comfort. She held him, her hands automatically cradling him, soothing him while she crooned reassurance.

Ben's big hands were on the knee now, wrapping round the joint, feeling for heat and swelling. Despite the size of his hands, Tassy noticed they were unbelievably gentle. His examination was brief and yet thorough, and when it was over he covered the child up again as if Sam's limbs were made of spun glass.

'Icepack and rest, as I imagine you're doing, and if it doesn't settle down in a while we can do something to relax the muscles a bit, to give you a break, eh, old-timer?'

Sam smiled wanly up at him. 'How long do I have to be here?' he asked plaintively.

'Till you're better. It takes different people different lengths of time, but we'll only keep you as long as you have to be here, especially if you're going to be horrid to my frogs and elephants.'

Sam's eyes, like Tassy's, tracked involuntarily to the tie again. 'Haven't you got any real ties?' Sam asked, his face a little puzzled. 'You know—navy or grey or dark red with little feathers on and things?'

Ben grinned. 'Yeah, I've got real ties. I wear them for job interviews.' He straightened up, those dratted eyes laughing again. 'Sister Franklin, I wonder if you'd do me the honour of showing me round the ward?'

Tassy's traitorous heart jerked as painfully as Sam's leg had done. 'Of course,' she said with a stab at graciousness. 'Sam, I'll be back in a minute with the cold pack.'

'Don't hurry—I hate it,' Sam told her with disgust. 'I want to get up.'

'You can't. You know that. Be good and I'll send Carol in to read to you—would you like that?'

He nodded slightly, and she smiled at him and resisted the urge to hug the brave little boy. Instead she waggled her fingers and followed Ben out of the room.

'He's a trouper,' Ben said softly. 'That leg must be giving him hell. Has he had a lot of joint involvement?'

'It's been intermittent, and it's getting better. It's been controlled until now, though. I think it's the fact that he can't rest it now because of the twitching that's making it so sore.'

Ben nodded, tapping his lips with one finger thoughtfully. Tassy, despite her intentions, found her eyes drawn helplessly to the soft fullness of his mouth and the firm, well-manicured finger tapping against it. Then he dropped his hand and turned towards her, and she was caught staring.

One eyebrow twitched, just oh so slightly, and she felt the slow burn of colour on her throat and cheeks. His smile, when it came, was gentle and understanding, which just made her furious. How dare he be so patronising and conciliatory? She glared at him, and his smile simply widened.

'About Sam,' she said through tight lips.

'Yes. Ice, sedation if he doesn't subside with treatment over the next hour or so, and lots of love and attention.' His brow creased. 'Where's Mum?'

'Working. She has a full-time job as a hairdresser and he's pretty self-sufficient. Dad isn't on the scene any more.'

His mouth tightened into a hard line, and for the first time Tassy saw the other side of him—the tough, uncompromising man who had made it his life to protect and defend the defenceless.

'People should have to pass an exam and sign a contract before they're allowed to conceive,' he muttered. 'So many kids from broken homes, single-parent families, foster-kids, kids in care—people are bastards.'

He sighed shortly and turned back to her, dredging up a smile that didn't reach his eyes. 'Sorry—hobbyhorse. Just tell me to shut up.'

Tassy shook her head, unable to conjure even a plastic smile. 'No way. I agree with you entirely. People never mean what they say any more. You can't trust anyone.'

'You can trust me,' he said, and her heart thumped and hiccuped and skidded around inside her ribs.

'That's what they all say,' she replied lightly. She turned into the kitchen and it shrank instantly to the size of a sardine tin, dwarfed by the presence of the big and very male man behind her. Trust him? Dammit, she couldn't trust herself! She opened the fridge door and pulled out a cold pack. 'I'll just put this on, then I'll find Carol to read to Sam.'

He followed her out. 'Who's Carol?'

'One of the patients. She's in for spinal fusion to correct scoliosis caused by spina bifida. She's had the op and she's now moving around again a bit, but she's very bored. She'll go home soon if they're happy with her.'

'And doesn't she mind spending time with him?'

Tassy grinned. 'No. She thinks he's great. He's got such a wicked sense of humour.'

'He doesn't like my ties,' Ben said mournfully, and Tassy laughed.

'You can hardly call that a character flaw,' she pointed out, and he chuckled.

'It does the trick, you know. Gives them something to think about. Instead of dreading my arrival, they wonder what tie I'm going to be wearing.'

She looked back at him, scanning the frogs, and had to admit that what they lacked in sartorial elegance they more than made up for in enthusiasm and amusement value. She smiled, meeting his eyes for the first time that day, and almost drowned in their gorgeous green depths. Her smile faded, chased away by a burning need that made her feel weak at the knees.

And talking of knees—

She was clutching Sam's cold pack to her chest and

it was icily unpleasant. Just what she needed to settle
her down. She ought to have a total body-wrap of the
stuff—

'I have to get on,' she said abruptly.

'Me, too. Happy with Sam? Give me a shout if you
think he needs any further medication.'

She nodded, went into the treatment room and found
a nurse to do the cold pack for Sam, then went on with
the rest of her work. There was a whole ward of children
needing her attention. She couldn't allow herself to get
distracted by that man and his unreasonably beautiful
eyes...

'Right. That's it, I am definitely going home!'

Josh laughed. 'It's only two hours after the end of
your shift, Tassy. Are you sure?'

'Positive. I'm going to go home, make a massive
sandwich and eat it in the bath!'

'Sounds good—oh, damn.' He picked up the phone in
answer to his bleeper, and with a little wave he left the
room, bound for A and E. Ben, sitting at the desk filling
in a child's notes, looked up and trapped her with those
eyes.

'Thanks for your help today,' he said quietly. 'I know
I've held you up and made you run behind time. I don't
suppose there's any point in offering to take you out for
a meal so you don't have to go home and cook?'

Tassy was tempted. Lord, she was tempted. She even
wavered for a second, but then she remembered all the
reasons why she shouldn't and she shook her head. 'No.
Sorry. I don't.'

'Don't what? Eat? I believe that's all I was offering.'

His softly spoken reprimand brought hated colour to

her cheeks yet again. Of course he didn't mean anything more. He wasn't interested in *her*. Whatever was she thinking about?

'I meant I don't go out with colleagues, for whatever reason,' she amended hastily.

'How about the hospital canteen?'

And have all those people watching them, talking about them, spreading rumours? Hardly.

'OK. Bad idea,' he said for her, his wry grin indicating that he had read her mind yet again. 'I just thought it would be nice to get out a bit—for both of us. I'm not exactly planning to jump your bones, Tassy.'

'I never thought you were,' she assured him. 'I just...'

'Don't?'

She nodded. 'I don't have a social life to speak of. I live very quietly in a tiny rented cottage, I mind my own business and keep very much to myself. I like it that way.'

'Because it's safe?'

She met his eyes defiantly. 'Yes, if you insist.'

'There's such a thing as being too safe, Tassy.'

Was there? Standing in the little office with his presence taking up so much of the space, she didn't agree. She wanted to be much, much safer than she felt at the moment. She grabbed her bag and pulled on her jacket, then headed for the door.

'I don't agree. Maureen's on now. She'll help you if you need her.'

'I've finished. I'm off myself now—let the SHO earn his keep.' He slapped the file closed, dropped it back into the trolley and stood up, stretching. His lemon-yellow shirt and dark green cords parted company, treating her to a peep of lean, taut abdomen rippling with muscle and arrowed with fine, dark hair under the dangling frogs, before he stuffed the shirt back into his waistband and snagged his jacket off the back of the chair. She dragged her eyes away and hauled in a lungful of air, before bolting from the room.

He followed her, falling in beside her in seconds, those long legs eating up the ground and easily keeping pace with her. Short of diving into the ladies' loo she was stuck with him, but she didn't have to like it or feel comfortable with it. She turned left in the corridor, then right at the end, through the door towards the car park and finally, when she thought he was going to walk her to her car, he hesitated at the exit.

'This is where we part company,' he said with a grin. 'If you're sure I can't persuade you?'

'Quite sure,' she said emphatically.

'Then I'll go back to my miserable little garret in the hospital accommodation block, and eat a packet of dry biscuits on my own.'

'Oh, shame,' she teased, but she didn't allow herself to relent or to be sucked in by the charming smile. 'I'm sure, if you ask, someone will share your biscuits.'

'Undoubtedly. Probably one of the rowdies who kept me awake all night. I don't suppose you know a good property rental company? I could do with somewhere to live that's a little quieter. I didn't sleep a wink last night—someone had a party. They finally settled down about four in the morning, I think.'

Tassy was on the point of referring him to the company she rented her own cottage from when she remembered that the one to which hers was attached was empty. The last tenants had moved out at the end of April and, as far as she knew, it was still vacant a month later. The last thing she needed was Ben next door, cluttering up her private life as well as her workplace. She'd have to keep him away from them.

'Sorry, I don't,' she lied. 'Try Verry and Partners in town. I understand they're good.'

He nodded, flashed her a smile and held the door for her, then vanished towards the accommodation block.

She felt a pang of guilt, but squashed it. He was wrong—it wasn't possible to be too safe, and having him right next door wouldn't feel safe at all! She drove home, let herself into her little cottage, put the kettle on and ran the bath. A long, hot soak, a cup of tea and a sandwich, followed by something undemanding on the television, she thought with a sigh of relief. Then maybe she'd be able to sleep without laughing green eyes tormenting her all night...

CHAPTER TWO

THE following day Tassy hardly saw Ben. He was busy all morning with Andrew Barrett in a paediatric clinic, and in the afternoon he spent some time in A and E with an emergency admission and followed the child to ITU.

It was an odd feeling, watching out for him, listening for his voice, hoping he would appear. She chastised herself for her silliness, but it didn't seem to stop her carrying on like a lovesick nitwit. She couldn't believe she was so stupid.

Apparently she wasn't the only one. 'Seen Dr Lazaar?' Sam asked her hopefully at lunchtime.

'No, not yet,' she told him. 'Why? Feeling rough?'

'Nah—just wondered what he'd got on his tie today.'

Tassy laughed softly. 'I thought you hated his ties.'

'I do—they just get worse. Expect it'll be spiders soon.'

Tassy shuddered. 'Hope not. How's your knee feeling?'

'Better—don't want any more ice. Is Carol busy?'

'I'll see,' she promised. She didn't want to overuse Carol's goodwill but, if she was willing to chat to the boy, it would pass the time for both of them. She went to look, and found the girl lying on her bed on her side, her eyes red-rimmed and bright with tears.

'Hey, sweetheart, what's the matter?' she asked gently, perching beside Carol and draping an arm over her shoulders—not that she could feel through the bulky

23

cast that held her spine straight while it healed. Tassy reached up and gently ruffled her hair. 'Down in the dumps?'

'I'm just so fed up. I seem to have spent my life in hospital, and I want to go home. Why did it have to be me?'

She turned into the pillow and sobbed, and Tassy squeezed her shoulder where it emerged from the cast and let her cry for a while. Then she got up and rinsed out Carol's flannel in cool water, and smoothed it over the hot, tear-tracked cheeks. 'There, now, that's better. Have you had lunch?'

Carol tried to shake her head but, of course, she couldn't, not with the cast holding it firmly facing forwards. 'Not hungry,' she mumbled.

'Let me find you something light—toast and tea? I haven't had anything yet—why don't you come into the kitchen with me and we'll have something together?' she coaxed.

The girl struggled up into a sitting position in her awkward cast, and slid her feet into her slippers. Tassy hugged her, smiled encouragingly and led her into the little kitchen. There was a small table against one wall, and Carol sat at it while Tassy made toast and put the kettle on.

She was just pouring water on the teabags when she heard Ben's voice. She nearly scalded herself, and set the kettle down and closed her eyes, counting to ten. Stupid, stupid, stupid! she chided herself. He's a man. You aren't interested. Forget it!

She passed Carol the tea, sat down and forced herself to coax and encourage the girl to eat and drink, ignoring the voice in the distance.

By the time their scant meal was finished and Carol had gone to talk to Sam the voice had vanished, and with it Tassy's patience. She did the drugs with her staff nurse, chatted to the children, settled a squabble and went in to Sam and Carol.

'Rabbits,' Sam said.

'Excuse me?'

'The tie—it was rabbits. Yucky blue rabbits—dozens of them, sitting in bright green lettuce.'

She smiled involuntarily. 'How cute.'

'Cute.' Sam stuck his fingers in his mouth and made a disgusting noise. Carol laughed and called him a foul child, and Sam poked his tongue out at her.

Tassy left them to it, a chuckle tickling at the back of her throat.

Blue rabbits, eh? The guy was nuts.

It was five-thirty and she was on her way home before she saw Ben and his blue rabbits near the exit to the car park. By this time the tie was tugged down, the top button was undone and he looked rough.

'Busy day?' she said sympathetically, despite herself.

'Just a tad. Still, it could have been worse. I thought we were going to lose him, but we didn't. At least not yet.'

'What was wrong?'

'Asthma—the usual story. Forgot his medication, went to play with a friend who had a cat—bingo. Friend's mum was a bit slow on the uptake as well. Still, he seems stable now.'

He glanced at his watch. 'I don't suppose you want to come house-hunting with me? I've got a couple of things to look at and I'm not sure where they are.'

'So ring the agent and ask for directions.'

'Is that a no?'

She smiled wryly. 'Yes, it's a no. I'm sorry, Ben.'

He shrugged and returned her wry smile. 'OK. I'll see you tomorrow.'

She went home, had a quick shower and went out in her tiny garden with a cup of tea and a little folding chair. It was wonderful—warm and sunny without being as hot as early June often was—and by that time of day it was perfect. She kicked off her shoes, wiggled her bare toes in the grass and sighed with delight.

Delicious. How could anyone live in the town? No wonder Ben had hated London—

Him again! She couldn't get through a thought without his name appearing in it! She gave him a mental glare and settled back to enjoy the sun. She wouldn't think about him.

She wouldn't...

He'd looked tired. Emotionally tired, the sort of tired you were when you'd been fighting death all day. There were days like that. It was why people went into paediatrics, and why they gave it up. If you lost too often, it got to you. Tassy knew. It had got to her a time or two, but then things would perk up and it would all be worth it again.

But he had looked tired. Perhaps he wasn't sleeping. She had a pang of guilt for not telling him about the next-door cottage, but then dismissed it. It was too close—too much.

And he was pushy.

And she was thinking about him again!

She got up and stomped inside. Why couldn't she just get on with her life like she had before the pesky man came along? She didn't have to sort out his housing arrangements—he was big enough and ugly enough to do that himself, without a helping hand from her!

She threw some pasta into boiling water, opened a jar of pesto and flung together a salad of sorts with her leftover bits and pieces. While she was busy she heard cars pull up onto the drive next door, and then doors opening and closing.

A new tenant? Good. It would be nice to have neighbours again. It had been a bit lonely here without any—a little isolated, even for Tassy. She listened, but all she could hear was the low rumble of two masculine voices. Oh, well, she'd find out soon enough.

She ate her supper in front of the television news, then cleared up and went back out into the garden to grab the last half-hour of sunshine. The cars had gone, she noticed. She wondered if the person had liked it and, if so, when they would move in, and if it would be a couple or just one person—or perhaps a family.

Not that it really mattered. If she saw as much of them as she had of the previous tenants, she would hardly recognise them in the street. If they were over-friendly, though, constantly hanging over the fence and chatting, lying in wait for her when she came home from work, it would be a real pain, especially if they were noisy. She'd had neighbours like that in the past, and it had driven her crazy. In fact, it had driven her out!

Still, whatever they were like, at least it meant that the house wasn't vacant any more and so she wouldn't have to wrestle with her conscience about Ben...

Ben was tired. He had been awake all night, worrying about the child in ITU, and it was taking its toll. Well, in fact he had been awake all night because the noisy individuals around him had been partying and yelling up and down the corridor until nearly four, and by then the urge to sleep had totally left him. The worrying had been something to do while he lay awake, as an alternative to thinking about Tassy.

Still, it wasn't for much longer. He'd found some-where to live now and he could move in just as soon as he could arrange to have his things delivered. They were in storage with a removal firm and he didn't suppose there was a cat in hell's chance of him getting them all by the weekend, but he wasn't sure he could stand an-other night like the last one.

He wondered where the line between murder and jus-tifiable homicide was drawn, and decided he'd probably be on the wrong side of it. Shame. It was one way of dealing with the nuisance.

Oh, well.

He flicked through the hanger holding his ties and rejected a couple, before settling on the teddies. Conventional Edward Bear types, they cavorted all over the sober navy background in varying states of disarray, bringing cheerful confusion to the neat rows of shelves they were supposed to be sitting on.

It was one of his more sensible ties for all that, less outrageous than most, but he didn't feel like pink el-ephants today.

He popped into ITU on his way to breakfast, to find that his young asthmatic patient was sleeping peacefully and had had a good night. With any luck the day would continue along the same lines…

None of them were that lucky. Not the nursing staff, not Ben and, most particularly, not the patients. Tassy was greeted by the information that her two qualified staff were off sick—one in the morning, one in the afternoon—which meant that as the only qualified member of staff on duty she had to get help from another ward to do drug rounds, difficult procedures and to cover herself for breaks.

It was easier, under the circumstances, not to have breaks, but it made a long and difficult day even more so.

Ben seemed to be tired and crotchety, she thought. He told her he'd found somewhere to live but that the firm storing his furniture were unable to deliver it until the middle of next week, and so he was going to have to stay in the hospital accommodation.

'Joy of joys,' he growled softly and, stretching out in the chair, he dropped his head back against the wall of her office and sighed hugely. 'I can't understand how they can all function on so little sleep. They never seem to go to bed at all.'

'Maybe they take it in turns to keep you awake,' Tassy suggested drily.

He snorted. 'Nothing would surprise me. Oh, well, it's not for much longer and I've got the weekend off. I expect I'll survive.'

Tassy, interested despite herself, was about to ask about his new place when his bleeper squawked. Simultaneously one of the junior nurses called her because a child was vomiting post-op and looking rather iffy, and the moment was lost.

The rest of the day was a blur.

The vomiting child became worse, Sam was fed up with his rheumatic fever pains and started to cry, and just when she'd got him settled down Carol slipped and fell and cracked her cast, hurt her back and had to be lifted very carefully onto her bed and taken down for X-ray to make sure she hadn't displaced the rod in her spine. Fortunately she hadn't so all Tassy's team had to do was make her comfortable and let her rest.

Then Ben came back up with a child on a trolley, collared her and whisked them both into the treatment room.

'Peritonitis,' he said succinctly. 'We need to get some fluids into her and check her blood, and empty that stomach so she doesn't keep retching, poor kid.'

Tassy looked at the 'poor kid' in question and felt her heart go out to her. She was about seven years old, thin and pale, her face clammy. 'Does she have a name?'

'Tracy Goodenough. Mum's on the way up—she's just signing consent forms and talking to Ross Hamilton. He's going to operate when she's rehydrated. He'll be up soon.'

Tassy bent over the little girl. 'Tracy? Can you hear me, sweetheart?' She brushed the damp fringe off her face and watched the heavy eyes flicker open warily. 'Tracy, we need to get some liquid inside you because you're a bit dried up after being so sick so we'll need to put a little needle in your arm, and we want to put a little tube down your throat into your tummy and empty it so you aren't sick any more—all right, darling? You'll soon feel much better then. Can you be brave for us?'

The little face wobbled for a second, then she nodded. 'Good girl,' Tassy said warmly. 'Right, you just lie there for a moment till we're ready, and then we'll soon have you much more comfortable.'

She hurried to get the trolleys laid with the things they would need, first for the intravenous line and blood tests and then for the nasogastric tube to empty her stomach. As soon as she was done she rejoined Ben, who was explaining to Tracy what he was going to do.

With Tassy holding the little arm steady, he pushed the needle into the vein on the back of the girl's hand, talking reassuringly to the child as he did so. Then he pushed the soft plastic cannula into the vein, withdrew the needle, taped the tube in place and connected the junction that would enable them to take blood, administer drugs and deliver the intravenous fluids without puncturing another vein. Throughout the whole procedure the child lay silent and unmoving, her eyes like saucers.

When it was over, the blood collected and labelled and the drip was connected and set up, she gave a little shaky sigh and closed her eyes. Tassy's gaze met Ben's.

'Gutsy,' he said softly. 'That's the trouble. Didn't like to make a fuss about the pain—apparently she's had it, on and off, for about a year.'

'Appendix?'

'Seems likely. That's what the surgeon thinks. Right, let's get the nasogastric tube in and then she won't feel sick any more. Tracy, my love, can we get you to sit up and lean on the pillows?'

He lifted her forwards gently while Tassy propped up the backrest, then measured the length of the tube against Tracy's chest and neck and wrapped a piece of tape round as a marker on it to make sure they inserted just enough. Then, giving her a glass of water and asking her to sip it and swallow, they eased the tube, lubricated with local anaesthetic gel, carefully up her nose and down her throat.

She gagged a little, but soon the marker was reached,

the tube was taped to her cheek and Tassy used a large syringe to withdraw the liquid from her stomach. As they finished Ross Hamilton came in followed by a worried young woman who was clutching a teddy bear like a lifeline, staring at her daughter with identical saucer-like eyes.

'This is Mrs Goodenough,' Ross introduced her. 'Now, Tracy, how are you feeling?'

'Sore,' she whispered.

'I'm sure. We'll soon have you feeling better.'

He checked the drip, calculated the level of pain relief and suggested intravenous ampicillin and metronidazole to start the antibiotic therapy. 'I'll see her at the end of this list—about five. That should give the fluids time to work and boost her a bit, and she'll be feeling a bit better.'

He left them and, with Mrs Goodenough trailing along unhappily behind, they transferred Tracy to a bed and left the two of them together while they prepared the notes and Ben wrote up the procedures and signed the drug chart.

'She looks awful,' Tassy said softly as they went into her office.

'She is awful. Her mother's racked with guilt, too. Apparently she told Tracy that if she didn't stop grumbling on about the pain she'd have to go to hospital for an operation. Now, of course, she's berating herself for not having taken it seriously enough. Still, it looks as though we've caught it in time.'

They went back out, talked to the mother again for a moment and then as Tassy was about to leave the bedside she heard Tracy say to Ben, 'You've got my teddy all over your tie!'

She smiled to herself. Another strike for the ties. She stayed on duty until Tracy was back from Theatre and stable, and then, exhausted but satisfied that the little girl was on the mend, she went home to find a strange car on the next-door drive and the front door hanging open.

As she got out of her car a man appeared in the doorway and hailed her. 'Tassy! You got my message—I didn't think you'd come.'

'Come?' she mumbled, staring blankly at him, her heart sinking.

He grinned, his mouth tipping in a lopsided, quirky smile that did something ridiculous to her legs. She braced herself against the car and tried not to notice how good he looked in those snug, well-worn jeans and the floppy T-shirt that was thoroughly past its sell-by date. His body shouted 'Hunk!' in letters ten feet high, and her own, hussy that it was, leapt to attention. She ignored it, still trying to work out the implications of his presence here—trying desperately to find another reason other than the obvious.

'You're my first visitor,' he was saying. 'I've moved in—decided I couldn't stand another night in that hellhole so I went to a furniture superstore, picked up a pine bed and brought it over. It's all I've got, apart from a kettle and a toothbrush, but it knocks spots off staying in the hospital another night.' He looked at her car.

'You'd better move that—you're on my neighbour's side.'

She shut the car door with a defeated thunk and sagged against it, her vain hopes descending in a tailspin. 'No, Ben, it's on my side. I *am* your neighbour.' She dredged up what she hoped was a smile. 'Welcome to Willow Cottage.'

His face was a picture. For a moment he looked stunned, then pleased, then a little wary. 'Um—did you know it was vacant and available to let?' he asked suspiciously.

'I thought they'd re-let it,' she fibbed.

'But you didn't mention it, just in case—is that right?'

He crossed over to her and stopped, although he could have crossed easily over the invisible line that divided the front garden. 'Tassy? Is it going to be a problem, my being here?'

She met his eyes reluctantly. 'I just thought if we were thrown together at work *and* at home—well, it might be a little oppressive.'

'You want me to move out?'

Out? No! she wanted to shout. He was so big and warm and solid—she'd be safe with him there. In a manner of speaking. She laughed breathlessly. 'Don't be crazy. We'll hardly be living together, after all. We're both so busy I doubt if we'll even see each other.' She turned away but her alter ego, the traitorous wretch, turned back and opened her mouth. 'Fancy a cup of tea?'

He was over the line and at her side in a flash, like an eager puppy just waiting for that one word of encouragement. His good-natured grin and easy camaraderie wiped out her protest before it was born. 'I thought you'd never offer,' he said with a smile, and the light evening breeze caught the scent of his skin, mingling it with the scent of honeysuckle to intoxicate her and dissolve the last of her self-control.

She led him into her little kitchen, then through into the sitting room that looked down over the valley through the French doors.

'This is lovely,' he said appreciatively, and then, just

as he had in her office, he prowled round, hefting the stone she had found in the stream below the garden, smoothing the piece of driftwood in the hearth, peering at the paintings, then crossing to the French doors which she had opened, breathing great lungfuls of fresh, scented air. 'No wonder you were so protective of it,' he said softly, and she forgave him his prowling because he loved her home and understood her feelings.

That made him even more dangerous.

She went back into the kitchen, put the kettle on and washed up her breakfast things while he prowled and fingered and sampled the textures. She might have known he'd be a tactile person. She'd bet her life he was a toucher, one of those people who thought nothing of grabbing your hand, squeezing your shoulder, patting your cheek—she did it herself with the children, but never with adults.

She just didn't feel comfortable doing it. Too unsure of her own welcome, she kept her distance. Ben would have no such scruples.

She made a big pot of tea, opened a packet of chocolate biscuits and went through to the sitting room. 'Have you eaten?'

He grinned and put down the book he was flicking through. 'In a manner of speaking. I grabbed some sandwiches on the way past a garage. Cotton wool and grass, I think they were—or was it meant to be salad?'

She shared his smile. 'Can I throw you something together?' she offered, wondering as she spoke what on earth she could throw, but he saved her from her unwarranted generosity and shook his head.

'No, thanks, the biscuits are fine. I'll go shopping tomorrow.' He looked around. 'So, the agent tells me the people who own the house divided off your end for her mother, and then she had to go into a home and they've moved with his job—is that right?'

Tassy nodded. 'He's only gone temporarily. A year or two, I think. That's why they're keeping it. They tacked on the bathroom and kitchen at the end for her mother, and it's fine for me. It's only tiny, but I don't need a lot of room. I haven't got many things.'

'So when did you move in?'

Tassy shook her head. 'Can't remember. Two years ago? About nine months before they went away, anyway.'

He put his mug down and looked her dead in the eye. 'Are you sure my presence here isn't going to be a problem?'

She returned his frank look with one of her own. 'Only if you make it one,' she told him honestly. 'If you leave me alone, don't crowd me, don't have wild parties and so on, I can't see it will be difficult.'

He grinned slowly. 'Wild parties? Tassy, I couldn't stay awake long enough to have a wild party at the moment.' His smile faded. 'I won't crowd you. In fact, I'll get out of your way now so you can cook yourself supper.'

He unfolded his long body from the chair, ducked through the sitting-room doorway into the kitchen and turned at the threshold. 'Thanks for the tea.'

'You're welcome. I hope you settle in all right. It can get a bit rowdy at night round here with the foxes and owls and so on, but at least they don't slam doors.'

His mouth tipped in a grin. 'I'll remember that when they're keeping me awake.' He hesitated a second. 'About that meal I owe you...'

'You don't owe me a meal.'

'Ah, well, there I beg to differ,' he said with a slow smile. 'If you won't take it the wrong way and feel crowded I'd like to take you out some time soon, just to say thank you for helping me settle in.'

She felt her heart flounder and get all girlish and excited. 'I don't think so—'

'Please? Pretty please with a cherry on top? I'll only feel beholden to you, and my ego can't cope with it.'

His disarming grin weakened her already shaky defences.

'Well—perhaps—maybe some time,' she conceded.

'That's what my mother used to say when she meant no.' The grin widened. 'So, is that no maybe or yes maybe?'

She couldn't help the little smile. 'That's just maybe, Ben.'

'Definitely maybe?'

She felt a little hiccup in the region of her heart. 'Definitely maybe,' she said firmly, and wondered why it felt as if she'd said yes.

'Progress, then,' he said, his lips twitching. 'We've gone from definitely no to definitely maybe. Things are looking up.'

She laughed and smacked his arm, instantly appalled at how easily she had touched him. She pulled away, but he followed her, closing the gap again. 'You've got chocolate on your lip,' he murmured, and a large, blunt-tipped finger came up and smudged the crumb away.

Then with a wink he turned, opened the door and went out, leaving her sagging weakly against the worktop.

For a moment there she'd been afraid he was going to kiss her. She closed her eyes and shook her head.

Kiss her? Why should he want to kiss her? Or take her out for dinner, except out of gratitude? She must be crazy to think it was anything else. He must be fighting women off with a stick!

She didn't pause too long to analyse the feeling that washed through her. It was altogether too much like disappointment...

CHAPTER THREE

BEN had so nearly kissed Tassy. He'd felt himself leaning forwards, felt the sharp tug of attraction, felt the jerk of his heart as his finger touched the soft, warm corner of her mouth.

He'd had to drag himself away, kicking and screaming, his body aching, his lips craving the touch of hers.

The night had been predictably hellish. The foxes had been out, the cubs howling and shrieking at each other, their blood-curdling cries shattering the night and reminding him of the fact that he was alone without a mate—without anyone to share life's trials and tribulations—and most specifically this night, when he was climbing walls after that kiss that hadn't happened.

The days were bad enough, watching her at work on the ward, her quick smile and gentle touch never directed at him. He had fantasies, though—Technicolor, full-blooded fantasies about that tender touch. And every day he watched her, fuelling his longings, driving himself nuts.

And now, by some freak of fate, some quirk of coincidence, he was living next to her, and her definitely no had changed to a definitely maybe.

Great. No parole for his sins. No let-up from the endless tormenting of his hormones. He'd listened to Josh and not pushed for a change in their relationship—even his dinner invitation had been carefully worded to be utterly innocuous—but he wasn't blind. She didn't like it, but she found herself drawn to him.

He could have kissed her. She would have let him. She probably would have keeled over and given him anything he'd asked for. He knew it would take only the slightest push to take them over the edge into a physical relationship, and he knew damn well she wasn't ready for that yet. Nor was he, not really. Not after the last time.

He showered—a nice hot shower. Cold showers, he'd discovered during the week, were a waste of time and just thoroughly unpleasant. So he had a hot one. Then he dressed and searched through the ties for one that seemed appropriate. He snatched it out of the case with a grim smile. Oh, yes, how very apt.

The fox in the henhouse.

He tied it, ran down the stairs, grabbed a sandwich and a glass of milk and left the house, trying hard not to look towards Tassy's windows. Was she dressed yet? Was she smoothing a rich, creamy lather over that smooth, milky skin? Massaging body lotion into those soft, womanly curves?

Hell, he'd be holed up in a garret writing poetry next! Disgusted with his lack of control and adolescent enthusiasm for a woman who was clearly not for him, he sighed heavily, stabbed his hands through his already tousled hair and tugged his tie down, loosening the top button of his shirt.

The damn chickens were going to choke him to death otherwise, if the fox didn't get them first…

Chickens. Big, fat, contented chickens on their perches, surrounded by fluffy yellow chicks scratching about on the floor, with a fox lurking on the knot watching them and licking his lips. Tassy bit her cheeks to stop the smile, but Sam thought the fox was funny and it coaxed the first laugh out of him she'd heard in days.

Tracy Goodenough liked it, too, and asked Tassy what she thought.

'Very amusing,' she teased Ben, tugging the tie, and he grinned and winked and let her get away with it.

'Was it the foxes last night that made you wear it?' she asked him during a lull.

He laughed softly. 'Damn things. I see what you mean about them being noisy.'

'It's only because they've got cubs. It's actually worse when they're mating, but it's the vixen that makes the awful din.'

'It's always the women that scream,' he said drily. 'Men have more dignity.'

Tassy, flushing slightly, gave him a dirty look. 'I wouldn't know. I'm not an expert on sexual responses.'

She walked off, her temper flaring for all sorts of reasons, not least that he had made her think—yet again—about him and sex in the same breath. Damn him. Living beside him was going to be a nightmare and, as if it wasn't already bad enough, she'd said she'd think about going out with him for a meal.

It's a duty meal, not because he wants to take you out, she reminded herself, but she would still have to endure it if she went, and her stupid relentlessly optimistic body wouldn't realise it was out of duty! Why, oh, why, hadn't she said no?

She went and found something distracting to do, which wasn't difficult. Carol was feeling very sorry for herself because her repaired cast wasn't as comfortable as before, and Sam was fed up and ranting about getting up, and the long-term orthopaedic patients were just about whizzing round the walls.

On top of that lot, they had a batch of new admissions for surgery—some as day cases, some for a longer stay—and they all had to be admitted and processed and checked and reassured and found time for.

Then a child was sent up from A and E with fever, swollen glands and dry skin on the face, hands and feet. '?Kawasaki disease' someone had written on the notes, and she admitted the little girl, noting the sheets of skin peeling off the hands and feet, the sore, red-rimmed eyes, the cracked lips and burning skin.

'We need to get her temperature down,' she told the parents. 'We'll take all her clothes off, sponge her with warm water and see if we can't make her more comfortable. I'll get a doctor to look at her now.'

She called Ben and he came in and smiled at the worried parents, scanned the notes, examined the child and wrote her up for soluble aspirin.

'I thought you shouldn't give aspirin to children,' the mother said worriedly.

'Only under certain conditions. How long has she been like this?'

'About a week or more,' the mother told them. 'I got the GP out three times and in the end he refused to come, even when I told him I thought she'd got Yamaha's disease. I just knew she had it.'

Ben's mouth twitched briefly. 'Kawasaki disease,' he corrected gently. 'Right idea, wrong bike manufacturer.'

The woman flapped her hand. 'Whatever. She has, hasn't she?'

Ben turned over the listless little hand and looked at

the sheet of skin peeling off it. 'Looks very much like it. We'll treat her as if she has, and then there's no danger of her developing heart disease as there would be if we ignored it.' He sat on the edge of the bed. 'So, when the GP saw her, what symptoms did she have?' he asked.

'Well, much the same.'

'Not as bad, of course,' her husband chipped in. 'She's got worse since he last saw her. It was only because the wife had seen something on the telly that we brought her to the hospital. It was the skin that made her think, you see. It's like a whole hand, or it will be when it comes off.'

Ben nodded. 'And did you tell the GP that?'

'Oh, yes. He wouldn't listen. Said a little knowledge was a dangerous thing and I should leave it to the professionals,' the woman said, her voice disgusted.

Tassy wondered how much or little knowledge the GP had that he was so unwilling to listen or to visit a child so young. The little girl was only two and a half.

Tassy removed the clothes carefully, comforted the child when she complained that it was cold and, covering her with a thin towel, she sponged her arms and legs and neck, concentrating on the areas where the blood vessels were close to the surface. The toddler had a digital thermometer under her arm, and every now and again Tassy checked it, reset it and put it back. After half an hour of sponging the child was slightly cooler, and she handed over to the mother, coming back to check at intervals.

She found Ben in the office on the phone to the GP, giving him grief. 'Ignorant bastard,' he said finally, slamming down the phone. 'He's an idiot! I can't believe he's qualified!'

'Maybe the parents weren't sufficiently articulate on the phone,' Tassy suggested. 'Unlike you. I hope he doesn't sue you.'

Ben gave her a withering look. 'For what? Telling the truth? I understood what they were saying.'

'But you'd seen her.'

'And, if they'd called me after I'd seen her three times and she wasn't getting better, would I have told them a little knowledge was a dangerous thing and leave it to the professionals?' He gave a disgusted snort. 'The man's a menace.'

He stalked out, went back to the child and her parents and announced himself satisfied that the temperature was starting to come down. Her condition was no longer deteriorating and he hoped she would now make a full and complete recovery very shortly. Then he left the ward, and Tassy continued to juggle all the many balls she had in the air at that moment until the end of the day.

Then she threw them all to Anna Long, the red-headed staff nurse who was now in charge, and made her escape.

She went home to find that Ben's car wasn't there. Her relief unaccountably tinged by disappointment, she went into her end of the house, kicked off her shoes, hauled off her uniform and had a cool shower, before pulling on shorts and a T-shirt and going out in the garden armed with a little trowel and a long, ice-cold glass of lemonade.

She weeded under the roses, stuck her nose inside one particularly inviting bloom and sighed with ecstasy. Wonderful. The scent, the texture—she loved them. She took another deep breath of the glorious perfume and then sat down, flopping back on the grass and staring

out over the valley stretched out ready for her enjoy-
ment.

Her eyes drifted shut, her ears still tuned to the buzz
of bees and the distant hum of traffic, and then gradually,
lulled by the warmth and scent and quiet sounds, she
slid into sleep.

Ben put a pizza in the oven, shoved all the rest of the
food he'd bought into the fridge or cupboards, threw
together a salad and went round to Tassy's door. She'd
say no, he was sure of it, but it was a lovely evening
and he didn't fancy sitting in the garden alone. He didn't
much fancy doing anything alone, but there you are.
Sometimes it just happens that way, he told himself, and
wondered why he seemed to be destined to spend so
much of his life alone.

Perhaps he ought to take up womanising.

With that in mind, he knocked again, but there was
still no reply. He resigned himself to a lonely meal, but
as he was turning away he caught sight of her stretched
out in the grass. Very quietly, so as not to disturb her,
he walked over towards her and then stopped.

Her long legs were bare all the way up to wherever,
her full, soft breasts under the T-shirt rising and falling
with her breathing, her eyelashes lying like black
sweeps' brushes against the pale, clear skin of her
cheeks. Her hair was loose and tousled, a collar-length
bob which yesterday had been still pinned up out of the
way. It looked soft and silky, and he wanted to run his
fingers through it. He wanted all sorts of things he
couldn't have.

He stood over her, watching her for a while, allowing
his fantasies a little rein, then, aware of how she would

feel about that, he backed carefully away, slammed his car door and called out cheerfully.

She sat up abruptly, startled and probably, unless he missed his guess, unimpressed with herself for falling asleep, and looked round over her shoulder at him.

'Oh—hi,' she replied, and scrambled to her feet, brushing the grass off her seat and knees and gathering up a glass and trowel from beside her. 'I was just weeding the roses.'

He couldn't stop the grin. She was flushed and flustered, and he thought she looked delectable. 'So I noticed,' he said drily.

She flushed a little more. 'Before I lay down. I was just listening to all the wonderful noises.'

Like him driving up, unloading the car, opening and shutting the house door, coming out again, knocking on her door—yeah. And he was the Pope.

'Which wonderful noises are those?' he asked, allowing her her little fib. 'The foxes?'

She laughed and wandered over to him. 'Did they annoy you so much?'

'Annoy? No. Disturb? Definitely. Look, have you eaten? I've just bunged a pizza in the oven and there's much too much for me. How about joining me?'

'Oh—I—er—'

'In the garden?' She hesitated, and he pressed his advantage ruthlessly. 'You'd be doing me a favour,' he lied. He could actually manage to eat the whole pizza without any trouble, but she didn't need to know that. She was weakening—he could tell. 'It's a deep-pan pizza with lots of extra toppings,' he tempted.

He could tell the moment she gave in. Her shoulders dropped a fraction, her mouth softened into a wry little quirk and she looked into his eyes. 'Ten minutes? I'll just go and put something else on.'

Disappointment slammed into him. He liked the shorts! 'You look fine—actually, I was just going to change into something similar.'

Her eyes widened a fraction—with alarm? 'OK,' she relented, but she still went into the house and shut the door.

He went and checked the pizza, taking it out of the oven in the nick of time, and dressed the salad before running upstairs, ripping off his clothes and rummaging through the case for shorts. The sooner he got his chest of drawers here the better. He found the shorts and a good long T-shirt to cover up any unseemly reactions, and ran back down just as she appeared at the door.

Her hair was brushed, her face washed, there was a trace of soft pink lipstick on her lips and she smelt wonderful.

He was suddenly very glad he'd put on the long T-shirt.

He looked incredible. Edible. And very male.

Oh, dear. This was a mistake.

Tassy sat down on the grass, her knees firmly pressed together, and watched as Ben brought out the food and set it down in front of her. The pizza was cut into big wedges, the salad was colourful and interesting and Ben was still the most appetising thing on the menu!

He sat beside her, handed her a plate and offered her the pizza. His big hairy knee brushed her thigh, and she forced herself not to flinch like a Victorian virgin. Instead, under the pretext of getting comfortable with her plate, she straightened her legs, which put them out of harm's way, and then instantly regretted the loss of contact. His leg had felt as good as it looked, firm and solid and warm and dependable.

Ridiculous. How could a leg be dependable?

They ate in companionable silence, looking down the garden at the valley stretched out in front of them, and she pointed out landmarks to him when he asked. Then he took her plate away, forbade her to move, made them some coffee and stretched out beside her on the grass again.

His eyes were shut and she examined his profile as he lay there. Strong. That was the word. His nose was straight and not too large, his chin was firm and decisive, with a slight cleft, his lips were just full enough to tempt without being lush, and his eyes—

Were open. Watching her.

Hot colour scorched her cheeks and she looked hastily away. 'I thought you'd gone to sleep.'

'So it was safe to look?'

'Look at what?' she asked with pretended nonchalance. He snorted, clearly unconvinced, and shifted so that he was lying on his side, facing her.

'Tassy, relax, I'm not about to bite you.'

Relax? Did he think she was mad? His hand came out and rested on her knee, and her leg jerked slightly. 'Tassy? Come on, lie down. Talk to me. Tell me about yourself.'

She laughed, a sad, hollow little sound without humour. 'There's really nothing to tell. Nothing you'd want to hear.'

'Try me.'

She stood up, brushing the grass off her legs and with it the tingle where his hand had rested. 'I don't think so,

Ben. Thank you for supper, it was lovely. I think I'll have an early night, if you don't mind.'

He let her go, to her surprise, and she bolted back to her hidey-hole and told herself she was being ridiculous. He'd had no intention of seducing her; it was perfectly innocent—

'Just like the fox on his tie,' she said disparagingly to herself. However nice he was, however kind and friendly and open, he was still a man on his own—single, healthy and presumably available.

Which she, she reminded herself, was not. Thank God she was on duty all over the weekend!

'So, how's our patient with Yamaha's?' he asked her with a grin.

She smiled back and tried not to stare at him. She hadn't seen him for days—he must have been away. Ridiculously, she'd missed him. She dragged her mind back to Lucy Baker. 'Better—much better. Mum's been here all weekend, sponging her off and on, and the aspirin, fluids and cooling seem to have got her under control. Her temperature's been normal since Sunday morning, and she's perky as a parrot now.'

'And how are you?'

She shrugged lightly. 'Fine. Have a good weekend off?'

He chuckled. 'Yes—I went home to my parents and got some good home cooking inside me. How's the weeding going?'

'I haven't had time. I'll have to finish it off on my day off tomorrow. Are you going to have a look at Lucy? She's probably ready to go home.'

'Yessir,' he quipped, snapped to attention and saluted.

Then one eye drooped in a sexy wink that did her blood pressure no good at all, and he vanished onto the ward, presumably to check his patient, while she tried to concentrate on finishing her drugs round.

Apart from the odd encounter with him, which kept her in a state of permanent hypertension, the day went smoothly for a change. Tracy Goodenough continued to make good progress after her appendicectomy, Lucy Baker, the little girl with Kawasaki disease, went home, Sam laughed a little and even Carol felt more cheerful because she was told she was going home soon as well.

Tassy went home too, a smile on her lips, threw some clothes into the little washing machine in her kitchen, pulled on her shorts and went outside to finish the rose bed.

She was interrupted by Ben, lounging against the little fence in the back garden that the owners had put up for the tenants, hailing her with a tall glass of something pale and cloudy.

She straightened up, scrubbed her hands on her bottom and wandered over.

'Here,' he said, and handed her the glass.

She eyed it suspiciously. 'What is it?'

'Home-made lemonade.'

She arched a disbelieving brow. 'Home-made by who?'

He looked wounded, then grinned. 'OK, my mother. I brought it back with me.'

She sniffed, sipped cautiously and then tipped the glass. Gorgeous. It was gorgeous. Not too tart, deliciously refreshing, blissfully cold—wow. She drained the glass and met his eyes. 'Yummy—thanks.'

'Mmm. Good, isn't it? That's why I went home! What are you doing?'

'Weeding. You've got a bit to do on your side as well.'

He glanced over his shoulder and nodded. 'So I see. Do you know a weed from a perennial?'

She chuckled. 'Not really. That's why I'm weeding the rose bed. I can tell the difference there—by and large the weeds don't attack you!'

'Roses won't attack you if you're careful.'

She snorted and handed him back the empty glass. 'Don't you believe it. Right, I must get on. I want to get this bit finished before it's dark. It's supposed to rain tomorrow.'

He hovered for a moment, then said, 'Want a hand?'

'With the weeding? It's very kind of you, but you've got your own to do.'

He grinned easily. 'That's all right, we can do that together as well. Less tedious if you've got good company.'

She couldn't disagree so she went back to her rose bed and he joined her moments later, his trousers replaced by shorts, his feet in old comfy-looking trainers without socks and his shirt discarded in favour of a much-loved T-shirt.

'Tell me what to do,' he said with an easy grin.

She laughed. 'What an invitation. You want to be careful—I might just take you up on it!'

He poked his tongue out at her, dropped to his knees and peered at the weedy earth. 'I take it we're aiming for brown bits in between the thorny bits.'

'Are you sure you aren't a presenter on a gardening programme?'

He lobbed a weed at her, then as she rose to her feet he leapt up and sprinted round the end of the bed, pausing there balanced on the balls of his feet, ready to feint in either direction.

She considered chasing him round the garden, weighed the possible implications of catching him and thought better of it. Instead she dropped back onto the grass, picked up her trowel and carried on weeding.

'Coward,' he taunted softly.

That did it. With surprising speed she sprang to her feet, darted round the end of the bed and launched herself after him. He ran, laughing, across the lawn, caught his foot in a loop of the hose and rolled headlong into a rose bush.

His howl of pain was spontaneous and absolutely genuine.

'Roses won't attack you if you're careful,' she mimicked cheerfully.

He rolled away from the bush, gave her a malevolent glower and stood up very carefully. 'Not funny,' he groaned.

It wasn't. She could see the tiny beads of blood seeping through his shirt from the scratches, and she imagined he might have the odd thorn stuck in his skin. 'I'd better have a look at you,' she said, feeling guilty now for being so callous.

'Can I trust you?'

'Probably not, but I'm your best option. We'd better get inside and sort you out—your place or mine?'

'Yours—I haven't got any first aid stuff yet.'

'And you a doctor?' she teased. 'Come on, then.'

She led the way in, told him to sit down and then had to bite her lips when he tried and couldn't.

'I seem to have a prickle or two in my backside,' he growled crossly.

'Oh, dear. Well, you'd better strip off and lie on the floor.'

She spread out a clean towel, helped him off with his T-shirt and then stood as he hesitated with his hand on the zip of his shorts.

'Go on, then. Take them off.'

He shrugged, slid the zip down and dropped them.

She couldn't help it.

She laughed. Laughed till she cried.

'What's so damn funny?' he growled.

She wheezed and wiped her eyes, unable to take her eyes off him. 'Your boxers,' she said with a chuckle, eyeing the little holly leaves that scampered all over the fabric with festive abandon. 'You must have had some subliminal realisation of what was going to happen. Oh, Lord, what a crease!' And she started to laugh again.

He glanced down, growled something unprintable and kicked his shorts aside, before lowering himself to the towel. 'Just don't hurt me for the hell of it,' he muttered, then dropped his head on his arms and left her to it.

She suppressed her laughter, looked carefully at his back and winced. 'Ow. It really did bite, didn't it?'

'Tell me about it,' he mumbled from the depths of his arms.

She started at the top, by the broad, well-muscled shoulders, and worked her way steadily down over the expanse of his shoulder-blades, round the deep curve of his ribs and across the trim waist to the top of his boxer shorts. She removed several thorns, some with tweezers, some with a fine needle, and then when she got to the boxer shorts she stopped.

'Finished?'

'I've finished your back.'

He lifted his hips, slid the boxers down over his firmly muscled bottom and rested his head on his arms again.

'I feel very vulnerable like this,' he mumbled.

She laughed, not altogether kindly, and tried to force herself to concentrate. It was very difficult, with all that wonderfully masculine man stretched out in front of her.

She picked up the tweezers, and he tensed, those finely honed muscles jumping in anticipation.

'Relax. I'm a nurse, remember?'

'I remember. Just you remember to be kind.'

'What's it worth?' she teased.

He shot her a dirty look over his shoulder, and with a rusty chuckle Tassy scraped together the ragged remains of her professionalism and tackled the last few thorns.

'I think that's all of them. Stay there while I get some antiseptic cream to rub into them.'

'What? Aren't you going to dab me with TCP or vinegar or some such savage little gem?'

'Don't tempt me,' she warned, rummaging in her first aid kit. 'Here—this won't hurt a bit.'

She smoothed the soothing cream over the whole of his back, massaging it gently into the sore areas, then worked up and down the strong columns of muscle that bracketed his spine. After a moment he groaned and she stopped. 'Does it hurt?' she asked, surprised.

He gave a grunt of laughter and lifted his head, looking at her sideways. 'Not exactly.'

'Oh.' Warmth crawled up her cheeks. So she wasn't the only one enjoying the feel of her hands on his skin.

'Perhaps I should have used the vinegar,' she joked a little breathlessly.

'Perhaps.' He hitched up his boxers, picked up his clothes as he stood up and held them strategically over the bits she was trying very hard not to look at. 'I'll go and put on something less prickly. Thank you.' And without another word he let himself out of the French doors, hopped over the fence and disappeared inside his kitchen.

Tassy sagged against the doorway, absently massaging the last trace of antiseptic cream into her fingers. Was it just her, or was he beautifully made? His muscles had rippled under the soft, satiny skin of his back, the solid bones just palpable underneath. He was lean and yet well built at the same time, strong and firm, substantial.

He would be heavy, she realised, and wondered how that weight would feel stretched out over her body—

A sharp, sudden ache of longing suffused her and she closed her eyes and whimpered. 'Damn you, Ben Lazaar. I was happy,' she said crossly. 'Now you've screwed everything up.'

She went inside, shut the door and cleared up the mess, trying not to think of that beautiful body lying stretched out across her carpet like a gift from the gods...

The next few days were difficult. Tassy avoided Ben like the plague, but he was impossible to avoid completely because they had, perforce, to work together, and he took every tiny opportunity to seek her out with his teasing grin and that slow, sexy wink that made her legs go all ridiculous, and whenever he thought he could get away with it he brushed against her.

He was a beast, and she was falling for his effortless charm like a lovestruck nitwit.

Then there were the times they were working together as a team on an emergency, and they made him even more irresistible because he was so focused, so professional and competent and skilled that he was a joy to work with. He never fumbled, he never hesitated except to consider, and then, having considered, he moved decisively to execute the next phase of treatment.

Even that level of skill, though, wasn't always enough.

On the Thursday of Ben's second week Heidi Crossley, a girl of eight, was admitted with vomiting, rash, high temperature and falling blood pressure. A and E had taken one look at her and admitted her immediately without further question because of her weakened state. Ben examined her, scanned the perfunctory notes from the A and E department and asked the parents for a history.

'She started vomiting on Tuesday night,' her mother said. 'About midnight or thereabouts. She was sick every half-hour or so until the morning, and I called the GP because she seemed so poorly.'

'What did he say when he saw her?' Ben asked, his fingers on her pulse.

'Well—nothing. He didn't see her. He said there was a bug about, and she would be fine in a few hours. Just keep her quiet.'

Ben nodded, and Tassy noticed a slight thinning of his lips. Oh, dear, another GP about to get a tonguelashing from him. 'So what happened then?' he asked.

'Well, she got worse. She got this rash all over her body, and she kept vomiting, and then she got diarrhoea, too, and I insisted he come out. He said she'd got sunburn—you could see from her skin that it was sunburn and not a rash—but it was on her hands and feet, and she was complaining of aches and pains in her muscles, and he said she'd probably got a virus as well—maybe German measles. He gave her something to stop her vomiting but she couldn't keep it down, and by this morning I was worried sick.'

'I'm not surprised,' Ben said, checking the child's cold, mottled extremities and studying the notes. 'Right, I want to get some fluids into her fast because she's very dehydrated, and I think we'll have her on a monitor, too, please, Sister Franklin. We'll get some bloods done, and I want to have a thorough look at her from end to end. Have her periods started?'

Mrs Crossley looked stunned. 'Good heavens, no. She's only eight. Why?'

Ben shook his head. 'Because the only other time I've seen symptoms like this was in a young woman with toxic shock syndrome caused by using tampons. If her periods haven't started that removes that possible source of infection so there must be another one. Has she cut herself, had any bites, burns—anything that might have become infected?'

While he talked and the parents thought hard about any possible wounds, Ben and Tassy were stripping off the child's clothes and checking her minutely for any possible site of infection.

They were halfway down her legs when Heidi's father said, 'She came in from the garden limping the other day. She had a splinter.'

They moved straight to her feet and, sure enough, in the instep of her left foot was a hot, red area with a hard rim.

'Here you go,' Ben said quietly. 'I'll bet you any money that's the site of infection. Right, first we need to get an intravenous line in to treat her for shock, then we need to open that up and swab it, check the blood and swab for Staphylococcus aureus and associated toxins. Then we need to start antibiotic therapy fast. What's her blood pressure?'

'Low. Seventy over forty.'

Ben swore softly under his breath. 'Right, fluids fast, and one hundred per cent oxygen while we do it. Better prepare for a cut-down just in case. Right, Mr and Mrs Crossley, I'm going to have to ask you to wait here while we take her into the treatment room for a few minutes. Once we've got her stable we'll bring her back in here and you can sit with her. All right?'

Tassy was already wheeling the child out of the isolation cubicle and heading for the treatment room. She heard Ben pause for a moment to reassure the parents and then he was beside her, helping her push the bed through and link the child up to oxygen.

'What are her chances?' Tassy asked him quietly.

He met her eyes, and the answer was there for her. 'We lost the woman with similar symptoms. Couldn't get her BP to pick up at all. In the end she arrested.'

'Oh, damn,' she said softly, and called Anna Long in to help them. Ben tried twice to get a line into first one arm, then the other, and finally he gave up and did the cut-down into a vein in her right ankle.

'Right, that's that,' he said, and as he removed enough blood for a battery of tests and put it into pre-warmed tubes to go to the lab the porter arrived to take them down, the fluids started to pour into the child's body and Ben was turning his attention to the foot.

They took a sample from the centre of the reddened area, where there was the beginnings of an abscess, and sent that off too for immediate analysis. Then, without waiting for the results, Ben started her on cloxacillin to treat the infection.

'How's her blood pressure now?' he asked.

Tassy, monitoring it out of the corner of her eye as she worked, shook her head. 'Falling slowly.'

'We'll have to set up an infusion pump. Gravity won't get it in fast enough. We'll need some plasma—30 mls per kilogram of body weight. What does she weigh?'

Tassy shrugged. 'I'll ask the mother.'

She slipped out and found the parents huddled together tearfully in the room they had been left in. She pulled up a chair. 'Mrs Crossley, do you happen to know what Heidi weighs? We need to know to get the drug strength right—an approximate idea will do.'

'Oh—about four and a half stone, I think—just over?'

'Thanks.' She gave them a reassuring smile. 'We've got the drip up, the samples have all gone off to the lab and we've started antibiotic therapy. You can see her in a minute.'

She went back to Ben, doing mental arithmetic all the way. 'About thirty kilos.'

'That's what I reckoned. Right. She needs 900 mls of plasma as fast as we can get it into her, and then all we can do is stand back and wait.'

'And if she doesn't pick up?'

'We'll put in a central venous pressure line, run in more plasma, give her IV hydrocortisone and just hope.'

He stabbed his hands through his hair and glowered at the child. 'Come on, damn you, you're going to get better.'

The plasma was running in now, bulking up her circulation. With any luck her hands and feet would start to turn pink again soon.

He picked up the notes and scanned them again, and then his eyes seemed to fasten on something. He swore softly and not very prettily, and Tassy stepped forward to see what he had found that had put such a murderous look in his eyes.

'It's the same GP—the same damned lunatic that nearly killed off Lucy Baker! Dammit, Tassy, this has gone far enough. It needs investigating.'

She nodded. 'I'll get medical records to run a computer check of the patients admitted who were being treated by him. It would be interesting to see if there was an increased incidence of anything nasty.'

'What—like death?'

'Exactly.'

He glanced back at Heidi. 'He's not having this one. How's her BP now?'

They leant over the monitor and frowned. 'No further drop,' Tassy said thoughtfully.

'But it's not picking up. Should we put in a CVP yet?'

She waited. It was a rhetorical question, and she knew Ben would answer it in his own time.

'Yes, I think so. Tassy, I want her in ITU. She's too unstable, too low to be treated on the ward. We don't have the facilities and you don't have the nursing staff to give the necessary cover.'

He left the room and came back a few minutes later.

'No beds,' he growled.

'I'll contact the nurse manager and get more staff—we'll look after her, Ben. We can do it if we have to.'

'Not that it will make much difference,' he said heavily, glaring at the monitor. 'Let's do the CVP line and get the hydorcortisone into her. Oh, and I think we ought to call Andrew Barrett.'

Tassy nodded. Looking at the child, she knew they'd need all the help they could get. Andrew arrived within five minutes, checked and confirmed the treatment so far and spoke to the parents. Then he came back to the treatment room and they took the child away to insert the line with X-ray backup.

She never returned to the ward. After nearly an hour, by which time Tassy was wondering what on earth could have happened and the parents were nearly out of their minds with worry, Andrew and Ben came back.

There was no need to ask them what had happened but she did anyway, after the parents had left in the company of a hospital social worker.

'She arrested,' Ben said tautly. 'We tried, but we couldn't get her back.'

Tassy turned away, her eyes filling with tears. 'Damn,' she whispered.

'I want that GP's blood, Tassy. He killed her. I want him hung, drawn and quartered.'

'It won't bring her back.'

'No, but it might stop any other kids dying unnecessarily, and if I can achieve that I will.'

He dropped Heidi Crossley's notes back on the desk and walked quietly out of the room.

CHAPTER FOUR

BEN couldn't relax. He'd spent the rest of the day chasing Medical Records in between patients, and with nothing further to achieve he'd come home to find Tassy out and nothing to take his mind off Heidi.

As the lesser of two evils, he turned his attention to the boxes that had now been delivered together with the rest of his furniture. Some he had labelled—crockery, pans, pictures and so on. Some hadn't been opened since—well, since they had been packed in a hurry a year ago.

They'd been in store, and he couldn't for the life of him remember what was in them apart from memories he wasn't sure he wanted to face. He poured himself a glass of whisky, sat down on the edge of the settee and pulled the first box towards him. With a deep breath he pulled off the packing tape and opened the flaps of the box.

Carla. Damn. He lifted out the signed, silver-framed photo and stared sightlessly at it. She'd given it to him the first time he'd met her, when he'd gone backstage with a friend who knew her.

'Ben,' she'd scrawled in her slashing, dramatic script. 'My love, Carla Fanzini.' Not 'best wishes', like anybody else would have put, but 'love'. What an empty promise that had turned out to be.

He focused on the picture, on the clean, sharp lines of her profile, the fine, slender nose, the delicate chin, the soft, full lips—and the eyes, those wonderfully dramatic eyes which had sought him out in the audience whenever he'd been able to get to a performance.

He put the picture down and picked up another, this time of her leaping through the air in a flurry of diaphanous gauze. Amazing, what the human body could be made to do. He put it aside and pulled out some other things—ornaments, programmes, bits and pieces that were just Carla. Did he need them? Was there any point in keeping them now?

There was a video of her performing in *Swan Lake* at Covent Garden, and he shoved it into the player and watched her while he chugged his Scotch and wallowed in self-pity. After a while he stopped watching his ex-lover and watched the performer, the highly skilled, beautifully honed machine that twirled and leapt and hovered, her body so graceful one would never believe its strength.

Perhaps she'd been right. Perhaps we did have a duty to use our gift, whatever that gift might be. He was using his. Perhaps she had a right to use hers, even if that did mean denying herself—and him—the children he had so longed for.

They would never have had a normal married life. Not like his parents, or his little sister and her husband with their new baby—not for Carla the night feeds and trips to the supermarket with the baby in the trolley and the dog in the car.

There was a knock at the front door, and he went and opened it. It was Tassy, her eyes wide and unhappy and her arms hugging her waist.

'Are you busy?'

He looked over his shoulder at the chaos and gave a

hollow smile. 'Not exactly. Just revisiting my past. Come in.'

He stepped back and Tassy followed him into the room, her eyes going to the television. 'Are you watching that?' she asked, her hands twisted together.

'No, it's a video.'

'I didn't know you liked ballet.'

He gave a little humourless laugh. 'I don't especially.'

Her face creased in confusion. 'So why are you watching it?'

'Just someone I used to know,' he said, suddenly uncomfortable. He crossed to the settee and picked up the remote control, flicking the video off. 'Better?'

She sat down carefully in amongst the pictures and programmes. 'Just someone you used to know?' she asked softly.

He sighed. He was going to have to tell her. 'Her name is Carla Fanzini—'

'I know. I recognised her. My mother's an ardent fan.' She met his eyes. 'Were you—? Was she—?'

'We lived together for four years. We split up a year ago—she, ah, had different ambitions, different things she needed to do with her life.'

'Such as?'

His laugh sounded harsh, even to his ears. 'Let's just say they didn't include me.'

Tassy picked up the pictures and looked at them, a strange expression on her face. 'She's very beautiful.'

Ben remembered the sharply cut lines of her face, the thin, muscular body, the tiredness that showed when she wasn't wearing make-up. 'I suppose she is, if that sort of thing appeals to you.'

'Oh, Ben, come on.'

He shook his head. 'I loved her, Tassy. I felt sorry for her. She was lonely, exhausted, and so was I. Her looks were nothing to do with it.'

'And pigs fly.'

'Really.' He moved the pictures and sat down beside her, taking her hands in his. He didn't really understand why, but it seemed important that she believed him. 'Her body was just a machine to her, a tool for her trade. Without it she would have had nothing. She'd made ballet her entire life and that was all she had at the end, all she could make room for. It was very sad, really.'

'My mother wanted me to be a ballerina,' she told him suddenly after a long moment of silence. 'Then I started to grow, and just went on and on and on upwards. The trouble was, I didn't go out, just up, so I ended up with what my mother called ''Wednesday legs''—as in ''When's dey legs gonna break?'''

He chuckled and she pulled her hands away. 'It wasn't funny. She was furious with me for growing, and then she started to tell me if I wasn't so thin it wouldn't be so bad—so I started to eat, and I ate and ate until I was fat, and then my bust grew like my legs had until she told me it was a good job my feet were so big or I'd fall over on my nose.'

'Your mother said that?' he asked incredulously.

She shrugged, an almost unnoticeable lift of one shoulder—a dismissive little gesture that hid, he was sure, a wealth of pain. 'Only jokingly. My mother has a strange sense of humour.'

Ben felt a huge wave of protectiveness sweep over him and, putting an arm round her shoulder, he pulled her up against him and hugged her gently. 'She certainly does. Tassy, you're lovely. There's nothing wrong with your body.'

She went stiff in his arms. 'Ben, don't patronise,' she said tightly. 'I know quite well what my body's like. I've had it for twenty-seven years, and I don't need you bolstering my ego by telling me lies. I know there's nothing wrong with it. It's healthy, it's strong and everything works, but it isn't lovely.'

'We'll have to agree to differ,' he said softly, letting her go and eyeing her with what he sincerely hoped didn't look like lust. That hug had proved to him what he had already suspected—she felt fantastic in his arms, and his unruly body was more than ready to grab her back and hang on.

He folded his arms to keep them under control and said quietly, in a matter-of-fact voice, 'At least you're a real woman. At least making love to you wouldn't be like making love to a steel hawser.'

Her eyes flew open and she stared at him, soft colour flooding her cheeks. 'Steel—? But she's lovely. Really lovely. So feminine—so agile. I would have thought...' She floundered to a halt, clearly embarrassed by what she had almost said.

Ben gave a hollow, sad little laugh as he remembered. 'No. She's a fantastic dancer, an exquisite performer, but as a lover—' He broke off. There had been nothing soft about her, nothing yielding, nothing womanly. She was too well honed—she had to be to do her job, and her mental focus was the same. Besides, more often than not they had both been too tired for more than a cursory coupling. 'It was just another exercise to be gone through,' he said quietly. 'She was a dancer, first and foremost, to the exclusion of everything else. And in the end it destroyed us.'

She reached out a hand and touched his cheek, and heat flooded him. 'Are you still sad?'

He thought for a moment, then shook his head slightly. 'No. Not any more. Life moves on. I was just going through these boxes to see what was in them, really. I'll probably just seal them up and put them in the spare room.'

His hand came up and wrapped over hers, and he turned towards her. That haunted look still hovered in the back of her eyes and, without thinking, his thumb caressed her soft, pale cheek. 'Are you OK? Did you need anything?'

Her shoulders lifted in a little shrug. 'I couldn't sleep. I went to bed and got up again, and went out in the garden. Then I saw your lights on and I thought—well, I don't know what I thought, really. I just didn't want to be on my own.'

'Heidi?'

She nodded, her lips caught in her teeth and then a shudder ran through her. He pulled her into his arms and lay back in the settee so she was cradled against his chest and he could stroke her and soothe her while she wept.

She was lucky, he thought. He was too angry to weep, too frustrated and wound up about Heidi's wasted life to let go and give in to the healing tears, so he held her and mumbled nothings and buried his nose in her hair and thought how good she felt in his arms—strong and solid and robust, and yet soft and warm and womanly and absolutely right.

And when she lifted her head his own came down and his lips found hers and clung to their sweet softness, and he forgot all about Heidi, and Carla, and all the good reasons they shouldn't be doing this, and lost himself in the magic of that first kiss...

It was a relatively innocent kiss, she supposed, as kisses went. His hands behaved themselves—well, more or less—and so did hers, except to slide round his back and hang on for dear life.

His mouth trapped hers as surely as if they were padlocked together, and for the life of her she couldn't have stopped him.

It was just as well, then, she thought later, that he'd stopped anyway. Not that she appreciated it at the time. She gave a little moan and arched against him, and he cupped her shoulders gently but firmly and eased away from her again.

'No, Tassy. This is crazy,' he murmured, and she wasn't sure if she imagined it or if his voice sounded a little ragged. It was hard to tell. The blood was singing in her ears and she could hardly focus. She pushed herself up and tugged her T-shirt straight, and wondered when the tingling in her body was going to stop or if she was destined to tingle for ever.

Then he tipped her chin, dropped another, very chaste kiss on her lips and ruffled her hair. 'Attagirl,' he said, and, yes, he did sound ragged.

She looked at him searchingly, and saw heat and longing and regret in his eyes, but before she could reach out to him and pull him down and beg him to take away the relentless tingle he stood up and crossed over to the French doors, stepping out into the night.

'How about a walk?' he suggested in that scrapy, unused voice, and she got up on legs that weren't any too steady and followed him out of the door.

They wandered round the garden and through the fence at the end that led out to the field at the bottom, and in the weak moonlight they strolled down over the meadow to the little river at the bottom of the valley.

It was wonderfully romantic—or it would have been if she hadn't felt so tongue-tied and if Ben hadn't been so remote.

'They're trying to trace him,' he said suddenly. 'They don't seem to be able to find any record of him in the area. He's doing long-term locum but apart from recent admissions nobody's heard of him.'

'So?'

'So they're wondering if he's a fraud—one of these non-doctors that acquire a certain amount of knowledge and then wangle themselves into a practice and kill people off.'

Tassy felt the blood drain out of her face. 'But how many others has he endangered?' she asked, shocked.

'Exactly. How many others has he killed?'

'It might be a red herring. He might be perfectly legit—'

'In which case he needs to be struck off.'

Tassy agreed silently. Anyone who was so dismissive of parents' worries and was proved so repeatedly wrong begged investigation. From the sound of it Ben was going to make sure he got it.

They walked on a little way along the river-bank, and just when they were about to turn back a dog bounded up to them, wuffing cheerfully.

It was sodden, filthy and extremely happy, and it was quite determined to say hello. Ben pounced just as it leapt up at Tassy, and buried his fingers in the soft, thick fur at the back of its neck.

'Down,' he said firmly, and the dog dropped to the ground and wiggled ingratiatingly.

Tassy eyed it with curiosity. It was impossible to tell its breed or colour, but she would hazard a guess at some sort of retriever. 'It looks like a well dog under the filth—has it got a collar?' she asked Ben, and he poked about in the thick ruff and came up with a tag.

'Ben,' he said. 'God, it's named after me. I'm not sure I'm flattered—have you smelt it?'

Tassy laughed. 'It's hard not to. Is there an address?'

'Bridge Cottage—that must be the one just along here on the lane.'

'Old Mrs Gates. She's got two dogs—they always bark when you walk past, but they're real softies. Golden retrievers—heavens, you'd never tell it was one of them! We ought to take it back.'

Ben eyed the dog, undid his belt with one hand and threaded it through the muddy collar, wrapped the other end round his hand and gave the dog a stern look. 'Now listen up, Ben. You are going to walk nicely—is that clear? No pulling. Right. Ben, heel!'

He set off with his left foot, the dog falling in obediently beside him.

Tassy blinked. 'Good grief. What a civilised dog!'

'He's been to obedience classes. I thought so when I said, "Down," and he dropped to the deck.'

'Maybe he just forgot the lesson about coming home clean,' Tassy said drily, and Ben chuckled.

They followed the path along the river-bank, and as they drew near the end they could hear someone calling feebly.

'Ben? Bad dog, come here!' the thin voice warbled.

The dog's ears pricked and he started to tug on the lead, but he was no match for his namesake. 'No way am I letting you off, you stinking rascal,' Ben said affectionately, and with another heel command he kept the dog in check until they arrived at the back fence of the cottage.

An elderly and rather frail woman was standing on the path, peering at them through the moonlight.

'Who's that?' she quavered nervously.

Tassy recognised her from chats over the fence. 'Mrs Gates? It's Tassy Franklin. We've got Ben—he's a bit muddy.'

'Oh, thank God—is he all right, Tassy?'

'Yes—can we come in?'

'Oh, do—can you manage the gate? Only my legs aren't so good these days and I've been up for hours calling him, the rascal.'

'We're fine,' Ben assured her, and once the dog was through the gate he let him off the lead.

Unrepentant, he bounded up to Mrs Gates, swiped her hand with his muddy tongue and grinned, before lolloping off to join the other dog sniffing about in the flowerbeds. 'Oh, my goodness, he smells dreadful,' she said, gazing after him in dismay. 'I'm so sorry you had all this trouble. Ben, you're a naughty boy!'

Ben didn't look exactly troubled but, then, the reprimand was very gently voiced and with such a wealth of love it didn't sound much like a threat.

'He could do with a bath,' Ben said from beside Tassy. 'Would you like us to do it to save you having to struggle with him?'

'Oh, would you? You'll get filthy, though. Perhaps I could just shut him in the kitchen, only he hates it—'

'We'll do it—we don't mind at all,' Ben said firmly, and Tassy wondered how much of this bath she was going to have to get involved in, and what colour her white T-shirt would end up. Still, there was no way Mrs Gates could manage, not with her arthritic hips. She led the way through the back door and pointed them at the bathroom off to the left. It was a nice little room, white mainly, and Tassy groaned at the thought of what they'd have to do to return it to its present pristine condition after the dog's bath.

Both Bens, however, seemed unfazed. One turned on the bathwater, the other sniffed happily about and grinned. It was obviously not the first time. The other dog, whose name, predictably, was Bill, made himself scarce.

'I'll put the kettle on—I expect you could do with a cuppa,' Mrs Gates was saying from the kitchen.

'Well, it's rather late—are you sure?' Tassy said, worried that they were keeping her up. It was after midnight, she was sure.

Mrs Gates laughed. 'My dear, I never sleep any more. I hurt too much. Still, it's not for much longer. I'm having my hips done in a couple of weeks, and then I should be better.'

'Both of them?' Tassy asked, surprised.

'Well, they thought it was easiest. They're both bad, and I can get all the recovery done and dusted and get back to normal quicker, they thought, than if they just did one and the other was still bad. I know they don't usually.'

She looked at Bill, sprawled in the corner of the

kitchen with his eyes shut, and shook her head. 'They're the real worry. I'm going to have to give them up and ask the RSPCA to re-home them, I think, because I don't know if I'll ever be able to look after them again.'

Tassy could see the sadness in her eyes, but before she could respond there was a yell from the bathroom and she excused herself and went to see how the Bens were doing.

The bath was ready, and Ben the man had stripped off his shirt.

'Can you lift him?' Tassy asked.

He snorted. 'I can, but I don't want to. He's disgusting! Ben, in!' he commanded, pointing at the water, and without any further discussion the dog hopped into the tepid water, sat down and waited.

Mrs Gates appeared in the doorway. 'He's used to baths. He's such a mucky little pup he's had hundreds. Here.'

She handed Tassy an old saucepan without a handle, and Tassy gave it to Ben. He filled it, tipped the contents over the dog and worked the water into the mud.

'He'll lie down for you if you ask him—Ben, down,' Mrs Gates said firmly.

He lay down, his head just above the water, and stared at them soulfully while Ben washed him thoroughly, rinsed him in several changes of water and then advised them all to get out.

'He won't shake—Ben, outside!' Mrs Gates told him, and the dog hopped out of the bath, ran out of the back door and shook gloriously.

'It saves the walls,' Mrs Gates said with a rueful smile, and went back to make a pot of tea while Tassy helped with the clean-up in the bathroom.

'She's going to have to get rid of them when she has her hip replacements in a couple of weeks,' Tassy told him quietly. 'She seems very upset.'

'I'm sure she is. Does she want to get rid of them?'

'No, I don't suppose so at all, but what choice has she got? I don't suppose she could afford to put them in kennels for months.'

'No.' Ben looked thoughtful. 'My mother's just lost her dog. My father says they won't have another one, but I know they will. They just can't stand the thought of a puppy, but these two are so well-behaved—I wonder if she'd like them homed just for a while, until she sees if she wants them back?'

Tassy paused in her wiping of the bath. 'Do you think they'd have them?'

'I'm sure they would—and they only live the other side of Norwich so they could bring them down to visit her every now and again.'

It seemed ideal. They didn't discuss it with Mrs Gates because Ben didn't want to disappoint her if his parents said no, but on the way home in the moonlight they talked about it again. Then Ben told her about his childhood in the Norfolk countryside and how he'd loved it, and how much he'd hated London with its noise and dirt and chaos.

'It's not just the cars, either. It's having that many people around all the time, pushing and shoving and trying to be there first, wherever there is. Hideous.'

And now he was back in his beloved countryside, and in his element, Tassy thought. He looked quite happy streaked with mud from the dog, and with his jeans sodden around the thighs where the water had slopped over the edge of the bath.

He didn't smell too good, either, but Tassy didn't care. It was just wonderful being with him, walking along the lane together hand in hand in the silvery moonlight.

It was such a change to have male company, to feel relaxed and yet charged with energy and a strange, zinging tension that made her feel nervous in a rather exciting sort of way. Not that anything would come of it. Men didn't find her attractive when it came to the crunch.

At least Derek hadn't.

'What's wrong?'

'Wrong?' she asked, dragged back to the present by Ben's voice.

'Your hand went stiff, as if you were thinking about something distinctly unpleasant.'

Well, that was right! She turned and smiled at him. 'Sorry. I was miles away.'

His fingers squeezed hers and he smiled back. 'Don't apologise. Was I right?'

She gave a mirthless little laugh. 'Yes. I was thinking about my ex.'

'It seems to be the night for that,' he said softly. 'Let's look on the bright side, Tassy—at least we're still alive and healthy.' Unlike Heidi, he could have added, but the thought hung in the air, spoiling the romance of the moment.

It was just as well because Tassy was getting pitifully close to getting carried away by it, and that would never do. Ben might find her mildly attractive—he might even find her attractive enough to dally with for a little while, although it was unlikely—but that's all it would be, a dalliance.

And Tassy didn't want to be dallied with or used by

anyone ever again. Once in anybody's lifetime was surely enough…

'They want them.'

She looked up and found herself confronted by a tie smothered in images of Bugs Bunny, nonchalantly munching carrots. She squashed the smile.

'Who want what?'

'My parents.' He shrugged away from the doorpost and came into her office. 'They want the dogs—if not permanently, then at least until she's better. It'll take months, of course, and I think they're hoping she'll decide not to have them back.' He ran a finger under one of her eyes and tutted. 'You didn't get enough sleep, thanks to that ungracious mutt.'

'Not to mention having to stay and have tea with Mrs Gates. Have you told her your parents want them?'

He shook his head. 'No. I've only just spoken to them.'

'Medical Records rang you, by the way, about our GP friend. There's a disturbing incidence of fatalities and late admissions appearing—they've handed the information over to the BMA.'

'Have they, indeed?' he said softly. 'And I wonder what the illustrious British Medical Association will come up with? Not that it will bring Heidi back, or any of the others. Still, it might have stopped him. Right, must get on. Anything I need to know?'

She handed him a wodge of notes. 'These have come in overnight, been clerked and admitted, but they could do with more thorough follow-up. One you might have problems with—he's deaf.'

Ben rolled his eyes. 'Great.'

'Want me to help? I've done a signing course as part of my Duke of Edinburgh's Award—it's been remarkably useful.'

'Sure. Aren't his parents about?'

'Oh, yes,' she said breezily, 'but he won't have them here all the time—he's twelve, and I think it's beneath his dignity to have Mummy hanging about.'

Ben laughed, and Tassy felt warmth spread through her at the sound.

'What's wrong with him?' Ben asked.

'Gastroenteritis—he's not very happy. He's been sick off and on for hours, and he has relentless diarrhoea. I think he's eaten something he's not confessing to, but until his mother goes home we won't get the full story out of him.'

Ben chuckled. 'OK. Let's go and meet him. Who's his GP?'

She smiled. 'Not our friend.'

'Thank God for small mercies. Right, let's go.'

They found the boy, Andrew Harvey, bent over a paper 'hat', losing his stomach contents yet again. He looked thoroughly wretched, and Tassy was convinced it was something he'd eaten. There was just something about him, and about the shifty look in his eyes when she asked what he'd eaten, that rang alarm bells.

She spent the first few moments of the examination getting rid of his mother. 'Why don't you go and have something to eat and drink? The staff nurse over there will give you a ticket to take up to the canteen. We'll be busy with him for a few minutes, anyway, so you might as well grab the chance.'

'Oh—well, if you're sure you can manage. What about interpreting?'

Tassy signed her answer, and the woman's face relaxed and she smiled. 'All right. Thank you, it would be nice to stretch my legs a bit. We seem to have been here for hours.'

She went off, and as soon as she was out of sight Tassy turned to the boy. 'What have you eaten?' she asked him again in sign language.

He shrugged.

'I want to know. If you went to a café or something and ate contaminated food then other people could be sick. The place should be inspected.'

He shook his head feebly. 'Not café. Friend's house. We had some leftover chicken.'

'Chicken,' she told Ben. 'Did you heat it up?' Tassy asked Andrew.

He nodded miserably.

'Just warmed it?'

He nodded again.

'And is your friend sick?'

'I don't know.'

'Should I phone and ask?' she questioned, wondering why it was such a big deal that he and a friend had had some chicken.

'No. I'm not allowed to see him,' the boy replied. 'Bad influence.'

Just then Anna came up to her. 'We've got another one of these coming in—a Nicky Coulter.'

'Same age?'

Anna nodded. 'Same area, too. Might be connected.'

Tassy turned back to him. 'Is it Nicky?' she asked.

Panic flared in his eyes, giving Tassy her answer without his reply. It was enough. She'd try and discuss it with both of them, and then Andrew's mother was going to have to know about it.

They set up a drip, sent specimens off for culture and treated him for salmonella poisoning, Ben's almost certain diagnosis.

They were right. Both Andrew and his friend Nicky were suffering from salmonella poisoning and they were put together, much to Mrs Harvey's horror and distress.

'He's forbidden to see the child—the mother's, well, not a suitable influence,' Mrs Harvey hissed at Tassy. 'I simply can't sit here in the same room with her.'

'Mrs Harvey, that's not my problem,' Tassy told her firmly. 'Your son needs you, we need to nurse the boys in the same way and it makes sense to have them together. Anyway, we thought it would be nice for them to have company while they recover.'

'Nice?' she said through clenched teeth. 'The child's well off the rails.'

'Well, perhaps your Andrew can be a stable and sensible influence. Anyway, it seems to me that if the boy can be bothered to learn to sign, just to communicate with Andrew, he can't be all bad. Perhaps he's lonely.'

Mrs Harvey looked at her son, then at the other boy lying limply on the next bed, his mother anxiously stroking the back of his pale hand. She looked tired and fraught, and Tassy wondered what she did to make Mrs Harvey disapprove of her so much. She didn't have to wait long to find out.

'She's a night-club hostess,' Tassy was told in a whisper. 'Out all hours, doing goodness knows what.'

'Doing her best to keep them together, I expect, taking any job she can that will enable her to pay the bills,' Tassy suggested quietly. 'Not everyone has a loving and supportive husband, Mrs Harvey. I'm sure there's more than one side to this, and she obviously loves her son. That's something you both have in common.'

Mrs Harvey shuddered, as if the thought of having anything in common with Nicky Coulter's mother was too hideous to contemplate, but Tassy didn't have time to worry about it. What she allowed her son to do was her business, but Tassy couldn't arrange her ward so that Mrs Harvey didn't have to be offended by the presence of a night-club hostess and her extremely sick little son.

Nicky's mother cornered her a little while later, looking exhausted and anxious. 'He will be all right, won't he?' she asked desperately. 'I couldn't bear it if he died. We've been through hell recently, and he's all I've got. The Child Support Agency want me to tell them the name of his father, and because I won't they won't give us any help and we can't get Income Support so I have to go out to work—I suppose she told you what I do?'

'Mrs Coulter, it's none of my business what you do.'

'Miss Coulter. I'm not married—and I'm not a prostitute, either. I'm a hostess. I talk to people, dance with them. Nothing more. I won't. Some of the others do, but I can't. Maybe I'm just not desperate enough and I would to keep Nicky, but, please, God, I won't have to.'

'Have you tried getting a job in the daytime while Nicky's at school?' Tassy asked cautiously.

Miss Coulter laughed. 'Oh, yeah, but they're like gold dust. I haven't got any qualifications. I got pregnant in school—I was only fifteen when I had Nicky, and I was never very bright. That's why I got mixed up with his father, but we're free of him now, thank God, and I'm going to make sure it stays that way, for Nicky's sake, even if I have to work in that horrible club. I do my best for him, that's all I can do.'

'So who looks after him while you're at work?' Tassy prodded gently, not sure she wanted to know the answer.

'My neighbour. She keeps an ear out—we leave the flat doors open. We're at the top, together, and no one else comes up the stairs, except to us, so it's pretty safe.' She chewed her lip anxiously for a second. 'He's a good kid, Sister. He's only ten, but he washes up for me and keeps his room clean, and he never gives me any worry. Oh, God, I'll die if he doesn't get better...'

Tassy hugged the thin, shaking shoulders and let her cry. Judging by the sound of it, she'd been tough for long enough. Maybe while Nicky was in she'd be able to have a bit of a break. Tassy wondered what the father had done that had made them so afraid of him. Men could be complete bastards, she thought angrily.

Then Ben strode into her field of vision and winked at her in passing, and she remembered his face the night before when he'd told her about Carla and how sad he'd looked, and she reminded herself that not all men were bad, any more than women were always the victims.

Had he been very badly hurt?

She had the sudden urge to put her arms round him and comfort him, not Miss Coulter, and she chastised herself for her silliness.

He didn't need her. He'd probably seek comfort in the arms of someone much more willing to accommodate his needs—and much better qualified.

She patted Nicky's mother, sat her down, shoved a handful of tissues at her and made her a cup of tea, before going back to the ward to check her patients. That, at least, she was qualified to do...

CHAPTER FIVE

THE weekend dawned gloriously hot and sunny, a typical mid-June day with only the lightest breath of wind to cool the air. Tassy went out early into the garden and tackled the rest of her weeds so that she could spend the remainder of the weekend with a clean conscience.

Then, talking of a clean conscience, while he was out she went and tackled Ben's weeds in the pretty beds behind his part of the house, still feeling guilty about the rose thorns. Not that any of it had been her fault, but he had supposedly been helping her at the time and she'd left the hose lying about that he'd caught his foot in.

So she cleaned up his garden and her conscience simultaneously, and by lunchtime she was hot and bothered and ready for something cold and refreshing to drink. She straightened up from the last bed, and was delighted to see him standing at the door with two glasses of the pale, cloudy liquid she knew was his mother's lemonade.

'Lifesaver,' she said with a laugh, scrambling to her feet and tugging off her sticky rubber gloves. The glass felt wonderfully cold, and she rolled it around her forehead. If Ben hadn't been standing there she would have tucked it inside the neck of her T-shirt and rolled it against her chest, but she decided it would be rather provocative and she didn't want to provoke him.

Well, probably not.

She drank the lemonade and showed him what she'd done, and he told her off gently for being silly.

'It was my fault I fell over in the rose bush,' he reminded her. 'Nothing at all to do with you.'

'Except that I was chasing you.'

He laughed softly. 'If I'd had a scrap of sense I would have stood still and let you catch me.'

The air stopped in her lungs, and for a few seconds everything seemed to grind to a halt as his words hung in the air. Then he took the glass from her hand, put it down with his and drew her into his arms.

'I'm going to kiss you, Tassy,' he told her, and, before she could protest that she was hot and sweaty and he really didn't want to touch her, his lips were on hers and she couldn't even remember her name. With a little moan of surrender she sank into his arms, and he folded her in against him, imprinting his hard, virile body on hers like a brand.

She wriggled closer, whimpering with frustration, and then, before she could move or speak or argue, he scooped her up in his arms and carried her across the lawn.

'Ben!' she squealed, and he silenced her with a kiss. She felt something soft and cool trail over her skin, and then they were in shade, the soft dappled shade of the willow for which the cottage was named, and he was setting her down on the lush green grass and stretching out beside her.

His lips were on hers again, his leg heavy, anchoring her hips as one hand cradled the back of her head and the other swallowed one breast easily with the huge spread of his fingers.

She didn't mean to kiss him back. She actually meant

to argue, to tell him that it wasn't what they were supposed to be doing and she didn't do this sort of thing and she wasn't like that, but the soft velvety sweep of his tongue paralysed her protest in its tracks, and the gentle kneading of his fingers made her breasts tingle and ache, and under the hot, muscular influence of his thigh her body was coming to life in a way it never had before.

So she didn't argue, she didn't tell him anything, she just slid her fingers into the soft thickness of his hair and kissed him back as if her life depended on it. She didn't even feel the catch give on her bra, just the rightness of it as his hand touched the bare skin of her breasts and dragged tormentingly over the pebbled peaks.

She could feel the rough texture of his leg against her thigh where her wraparound skirt had unwrapped, and then the heat of his hand cupping her, making the ache so much worse she thought she'd weep with frustration.

'Ben?' she whispered against his lips.

He lifted his head a fraction. 'Tassy, I want you,' he breathed raggedly.

And that was it. Her resistance, feeble thing that it was, keeled over in the long grass and was lost from view as she reached up and drew him down again. 'I want you, too,' she confessed, unable to resist the pounding need that he'd created in her.

He moved a little, just enough so that he could undo his shorts and slide them down, kicking them away. He sat up and wrenched off his T-shirt, then turned back to her, gloriously naked and unashamedly aroused.

Tassy thought her heart was going to stop, she wanted him so badly. Then he touched her, pushing up her grubby weed-stained T-shirt, unravelling her skirt with trembling fingers, easing down the plain, serviceable cotton knickers that made her want to die of embarrassment. And then she forgot about her knickers, about the fact that she was absurdly top-heavy and she hated herself, because his hands were all over her, their touch so gentle, so careful, so generous, as if he really meant the whispered words that surrounded her in their leafy haven under the skirts of the willow.

Then his body was stretched out over hers and she felt the heavy, solid thrust of his need against the screaming ache he'd built in her, and she lifted herself to him and begged him to love her.

He moved, and a sharp, sudden pain made her eyes fly open and meet his. He froze, his face hovering over hers, his eyes puzzled. 'Tassy?' he whispered.

'Ben, please, just love me,' she pleaded. 'Don't ask—not now. Just love me.'

He hesitated for ages, his eyes searching hers, then with a ragged moan he lowered his mouth to hers, trapping the little cry of pain as he entered her. Miraculously the pain was gone, driven out by the wonderful fullness that was loving him, and she buried her face in his shoulder, wrapped her arms around him and gave in to the sensations that swamped her.

Ben couldn't believe it. A virgin. My God, he thought, she was a virgin and she gave herself to me.

A lump rose in his throat, and he had to choke down the ridiculous urge to cry. Instead he lifted his head a fraction and kissed her, oh, so softly on her bruised and swollen lips. 'Are you all right?' he said, and his voice was rough and scratchy round the edges. He searched her eyes, and found them soft and luminous with tears.

'I'm fine,' she whispered.

'Did I hurt you?'

She shook her head. 'Not really. Only for a second—less than that.'

'You should have told me.'

'Why? You would have stopped.'

He felt the smile coming. 'No, Tassy, I couldn't have stopped if my life had depended on it. Not then. But I wouldn't have done it here, like this, either.'

She looked around them at the pale canopy of the willow, trailing on the lush, fragrant grass like a living veil to hide them from the world, then met his eyes again. 'Why not? It was beautiful.'

'You were beautiful,' he told her, and felt that absurd urge to cry welling up in him again. 'You are beautiful.' He touched his lips to hers, squeezing his eyes shut so he didn't make a complete ass of himself.

Then he lifted his head, looked down at her again and didn't care if he did because the tears were welling gently from the corners of her eyes and sliding down into her hair.

'You really mean it, don't you?' she said tremulously, and he shook his head in despair and kissed her again.

'Of course I mean it. Dammit, Tassy, what do I have to do to prove it to you?'

She sniffed and smiled. 'I think you did. I still think you're wrong, but at least you're sincere. Just don't say you regret it.'

'Never. How could I regret it? No one's ever given me anything as precious as what you've just given me.'

Her eyes filled again. 'It wasn't precious,' she whispered, and his heart ached at the emptiness in her words.

'It was to me,' he assured her, his voice ragged again.

'You're just saying that.'

He opened his mouth to argue, but the wrong words came out—or perhaps they were the right ones. He smudged away her tears with his thumbs, kissed the tip of her nose and said unevenly, 'I love you, Tassy.'

She froze beneath him, then her breath jerked a little and she shook her head in denial. 'No,' she protested. 'No, you don't. Don't be silly—'

'I'm not being silly. I do love you.'

'You don't know me.'

'Yes, I do. I know you care enough to give me something you've never given anyone else.'

She laughed, a harsh, bitter sound that cut him like a knife. 'Not for want of trying. Even my husband didn't want it.'

He eased away from her and rolled to his back, taking her with him so that her head was cradled on his shoulder and his arms were round her, smoothing her silky skin with fingers that still shook from loving her. 'Tell me about it,' he said quietly.

For an age she was silent and he thought she wasn't going to tell him, but then she did, her voice halting and very soft so he had to strain to hear the words.

'He was a teacher. We'd known each other two weeks—the same length of time I've known you. He went for an interview for a headship at a prep school, and he came back and proposed to me. He said he'd loved me from the moment he'd set eyes on me, and now he'd got this wonderful job he was able to offer me a future. I didn't even know we had a future together, but he was very convincing and I was flattered. He was much older than me, nearly thirty-four to my twenty-one, and I was very gullible.'

Ben felt a murderous rage rise up inside him. 'Don't tell me—he'd been offered the job on condition he was married or about to be.'

Her smile was bleak and cut him to the bone. 'We didn't have a honeymoon—there wasn't time. We had to move in, and he went ahead without me while I finished off my training. By the time I joined him he'd been in the schoolhouse for two weeks and it was the start of term. He was quite stressed—it was a demanding job and he was finding it quite hard. Naturally he was tired at night—'

'Naturally,' Ben said under his breath.

'Anyway, he did try one night to make love to me and he just—well, he couldn't. He said he was too tired and stressed.'

'And?'

'And I believed him. I was an idiot. He strung me along until February, then I went over to the school at half-term because I needed to ask him something and I found him and his secretary, making out on the chair in his study. It was quite obvious he wasn't too tired or stressed to make love to her.'

She turned her face away and fiddled with the hair on his chest.

'So your marriage was annulled.'

'Yes. He lied and said I was frigid and wouldn't let him near me. As he had his secretary all lined up ready to say he was quite able to perform there didn't seem any point in arguing. All it would have proved was the truth, which was that he couldn't make love to me because he didn't find me attractive. It seemed perfectly reasonable. After all, I had Wednesday legs and this stupid chest and a face that never launched so much as a rubber dinghy—'

Ben laughed softly and hugged her, otherwise he would have lain there and cried for her. 'I love your Wednesday legs,' he told her. 'They're beautiful, and they go all the way up to here...'

He stroked his hand up her thigh, and she gasped and clamped her legs on his hand to stop it moving, so he moved his thumb instead, rotating it gently until she sighed softly and her legs relaxed, falling open for him.

'That's better,' he murmured. 'And as for this stupid chest...'

He levered himself up on one elbow and took the soft pink nipples in his mouth in turn, drawing on them and blowing lightly until they were puckered and reaching up to him.

'Ben,' she whispered, the sound half protest, half plea, so he listened to the plea and stretched himself over her again.

This time, when the tears filled his eyes he let them flow...

Tassy lay in the bath and stared at the ceiling and wondered what on earth she'd been thinking about. Not common-sense precautions, certainly. She wondered if her rats' nest of a brain had once dwelt on the possibility of pregnancy, and decided it probably hadn't. She'd been too busy being filled with nonsense about love and suchlike to pay attention to the basics.

Until, that is, Ben rolled away from her and pointed out that, unless there was something she hadn't told him, there were about sixty million opportunities for conception swimming about inside her.

Something deep and yearning and primitive had cried out to be heard at that point, but she'd suppressed it and fled to run a bath.

Not that it would do any good. There'd been plenty of time for a determined little sperm to swim all the way to France before they'd thought about it. The damage, if there was to be any, was probably well and truly done.

Still, the bathwater was lovely and soothing to her unaccustomed tenderness, and she felt hot and sticky and unattractive after all her gardening, so she was quite happy to lie there and wonder what on earth had possessed her to hurl herself at Ben quite so rapidly.

Two weeks—not even that! She must be nuts. What did she know about him, apart from the fact that he got very angry when children were hurt through neglect or malice and that he felt people should pass a test before they were allowed to conceive—and where had that conviction been at the psychological moment?

She'd heard his car go out a few moments ago, and now she heard it return. He'd probably gone to buy the paper—while she lay there, tortured by the most momentous thing to happen to her in her life—

'Tassy?'

'In the bath,' she called out.

She heard him pottering about in her kitchen, then a tap at the door. 'Can I come in?'

Ridiculous question as there wasn't a lock on the door, but at least it showed a certain measure of respect, Tassy supposed. Respect or not, it didn't get her away from the fact that she was going to have to look him in the eye again soon and she wasn't quite sure she could cope with it. She didn't have the first clue about protocol and sexual shenanigans, never having indulged in them, and she felt shy and gauche and adolescent.

She sat up in the bath and wrapped her arms over her very naked and vulnerable chest, and said very warily, 'Yes, I suppose so.'

The door swung open and a tray came in, followed by Ben clad only in a towel. 'Here,' he said, and handed her the tray so she had no option but to let go of her chest and take it.

His eyes hovered appreciatively in that vicinity for a second, and then he dropped the towel, climbed into the bath and folded himself up at the tap end.

Water slopped perilously close to the top, and she gave a little shriek as she felt something slide along her leg and up her thigh. 'Is that your foot?' she asked suspiciously.

He grinned and wiggled his toes, and she shot backwards with a little yelp and slopped water out of the end of the bath.

'My, aren't you skittish? Here, hand me the tray—it's covering up too much of you and I want to look at you.'

'Tough,' she said, hanging on like grim death. 'As far as I'm concerned, it couldn't possibly cover enough. What are you doing in my bath?'

He grinned again, clearly happy with himself. 'Sharing it—and I brought you lunch.'

'I don't normally share a bath with waiters,' she said haughtily, and he wiggled his toes again, which shut her up instantly.

'Here, help yourself,' he told her, and she looked down at the tray. There was a selection of dips surrounded by carrot and celery sticks, little tiny breadsticks and fat, thick-sliced crisps. She took a piece of carrot and swiped it through the nearest dip, and crunched it up. It was cool and refreshing and delicious, and after a few moments when Ben did nothing but eat and virtually ignore her she settled the tray more comfortably on her knees and tucked in.

It had been a trick, of course, she realised a moment later when she looked up and found his eyes on her. She blushed softly and looked down away from that teasing green gaze, only to find one blunt fingertip under her chin, lifting it gently so she was facing him again.

'You are beautiful, Tassy,' he told her quietly, and the sincerity in his voice and the fierce flame in his eyes gave her no choice but to believe he meant it.

And, foolish thing that she was, she lapped it up. He lifted the tray from her lap and set it on the floor, then stood up and pulled her to her feet and into his arms. He hugged her gently and then, setting her away from him, he washed her with tender intimacy while she blushed and gasped and wished she'd had the foresight, optimism and intelligence to go out and buy condoms.

When he'd finished he took her hands, put the soap in them and encouraged her to return the favour.

It was wonderful to explore his body, to feel the various textures and resiliences of the different areas. She got a little involved here and there, but he didn't seem to mind. In fact, he was getting quite into it himself, she thought with a little smile.

Then he stopped her, his hands stilling hers, and he rinsed them both off and helped her out of the bath, swathed her in her towel and pushed her out into the sitting room. He paused long enough to grab the lunch, then followed her out and chivvied her up the stairs to her bedroom.

'We can't,' she protested, but he just smiled and moved the crisps, and there in the bottom of the bowl was a little foil packet.

'I went shopping,' he said with a sly grin, 'so we can.'

They did—all night and the following morning, when they weren't stretched out across his new bed which was bigger than hers and better able to cope with both of them.

Then the phone rang, and Ben hooked on some shorts and ran downstairs to get it. Tassy curled on her side, sore and contented and wondering what she'd ever seen in Derek. Ben came back up, grinning like a Cheshire cat.

'Good news,' he told her without preamble. 'The agent has managed to get hold of the owners and they've accepted my offer.'

She pushed herself up into a sitting position and scraped her hair out of her eyes. 'What? What agent? What owners?'

'Of this place. I asked the agent if there was any likelihood they'd sell, and he said he'd try and find out. Apparently they've been offered the job on a permanent basis and so they were quite happy.'

Tassy looked at him blankly. 'So you're buying this house?'

'Yup.'

'Both halves?'

'Of course.'

'Oh.' She caught her lip in her teeth and gnawed at it for a moment. 'So you'll be my landlord?'

Ben gave her a funny look. 'Well—technically, I suppose. I hadn't got as far as thinking about that.'

Tassy felt suddenly terribly threatened. She'd always known her tenancy was strictly shorthold and that she could be asked to move at the end of the contract term, but she hadn't expected it to come out of the blue like this, or for it to be Ben.

He reached out and took one of her hands in his, his thumb idly caressing her pulse point. 'Tassy, is there a problem?'

She pulled her hand away. His touch was distracting her and she didn't want to be distracted. 'I don't know. Maybe. It's one thing you being a co-tenant, it's quite another being my landlord. It might not work.'

He took her hand back firmly. 'I would have thought after last night things were different anyway.'

She met his eyes and looked away again, suddenly feeling crowded. 'Why should they be?'

'Why?' His laugh was incredulous. 'Tassy, we're lovers. We've just spent the night together. I would have thought the sensible thing to do would be to open up the communicating doors and have the whole house—or let your part.'

'Move me in with you?'

'Yes.'

'Just like that, after two weeks?' Panic clawed at her. 'Ben, it's too soon. I don't know why I didn't stop you yesterday, but I probably should have done—'

'Don't tell me you regret it,' he said, throwing her own words back at her. She looked up at him and his eyes were guarded, shielding the hurt she knew he was feeling.

'I don't regret it,' she promised softly, 'but I don't want us to rush into anything too soon.'

'So stay in your part and we'll leave the doors until you feel ready.'

'And what if I don't?' she asked. 'What if I never feel ready?'

He shrugged. 'Let's cross that bridge if and when we get to it.'

She took her hand back again and scooted out of the bed, pulling on her clothes to cover her suddenly very naked body. 'I'll think about it,' she told him and, grabbing her shoes, she headed for the door.

'Tassy? What the hell are you doing?' he called after her.

She paused in the doorway, feeling guilty because of the things they'd shared and the way she was running now, but she had to have some space. 'Going back to my place—Ben, I need to think. I'll speak to you later.'

She felt his eyes on her as she crossed the little landing and went downstairs, then out of the door and round to her own door.

That was when she encountered the first hurdle. Her keys were in his house and she'd dropped the latch on his door as she came out. The only way she could get back in was to ring his bell and face him again, and suddenly it all seemed too much to cope with.

With a little howl of frustration she plonked herself down on the doorstep and dropped her face in her arms. How long she sat there she didn't know, but eventually she heard his footsteps, then she felt the firm pressure of his thigh against hers as he sat beside her.

'Tassy?' His voice was a low murmur, a gentle, coaxing sound that had her turning into his arms with a little sob. 'Oh, love, what a silly girl,' he said kindly and held her while the unexpected and foolish tears worked themselves out of her system.

After which, of course, she felt even more foolish. He mopped her up, gave her a kiss and pulled her to her feet, putting her keys into her hand. 'Go on, then, in you go and have a sleep. I expect you're tired.'

'Mmm,' she mumbled, suddenly aware of just how tired she was.

'Will I see you later?' he asked softly.

She lifted her shoulders in a little shrug. 'I don't know—maybe.'

His mouth quirked in a teasing smile. 'Is that another definitely maybe?'

She laughed despite herself. 'That's just a maybe, Ben. I'll see. I'm going to bed.'

'Think of me,' he murmured as her door closed on him. She trudged upstairs and dropped into her bed, without making it.

It was crumpled and chaotic, the way they'd left it, and she could smell the faintest trace of his aftershave on her pillow.

Think of him? There was no chance of her doing anything else!

CHAPTER SIX

TASSY woke up at four-thirty on Monday morning, refreshed but troubled. She had a bath, then made a cup of tea, opened the French doors and sat on the step in the cool morning air, considering the dramatic shift in her life.

Two days ago she'd been a virgin, a tenant and at peace with herself.

Now she was certainly not at peace, and most definitely not a virgin. The tenant bit she wasn't sure about but there were changes ahead, that was certain. She'd always hoped the owners would come back and allow her to continue to live there as they had before, but she supposed that was too much to hope for. Her second choice was that someone would buy the house as a rental investment, but that was unrealistic. Although it wasn't big, it would make a lovely family home if it was opened up again, and the setting was glorious.

She couldn't blame Ben for wanting to buy it, but as her thoughts crystallised she realised she was angry with him not for buying it but for not telling her about his plans. He could have shared it with her, especially considering the things they had done…

Her cheeks heated at the thought, and she had to force herself to remember that they hadn't really spent a great deal of time in conversation, and their relationship had taken a dramatic shift from platonic 'Hi, have a glass of lemonade' to 'I love you' in the space of about ten minutes. There hadn't been a lot of time to say, 'By the way, I'm thinking of putting in an offer on the cottage.'

She groaned and buried her head in her arms. How could he love her so soon? He'd said he'd been in love with Carla—how could he love her, then, so easily and so soon? Did he just imagine himself in love with every woman he met, or did he simply tell the women he made love to—and surely there must be hundreds—what he thought they wanted to hear?

Her own feelings she didn't dare dwell on because if she once admitted how much she loved him she'd fall apart when it was all over—and all over it would be, she was sure of that.

He'd get bored with her soft, lush body and Wednesday legs and start longing for his dainty little steel hawser again.

Or perhaps he'd just move on—

'Mind if I join you?'

She jumped almost out of her skin, and looked up to see Ben, lolling against the frame of his kitchen door, mug in hand.

'Feel free,' she said. 'After all, you own it.'

'Not yet.' He swung his legs over the fence and came and sat beside her on the step, eyeing her critically. 'How are you?'

'Better. I slept right through.'

'You needed to.' His hand came up and she felt the soft brush of his knuckles against her cheek. 'I missed you.'

She threw him a sceptical glance but his eyes weren't teasing this time—they were quiet and sincere. She looked away again and plucked up a piece of grass, shredding it in agitated fingers. She'd missed him, too, but he'd have to put her on the rack to get her to confess to it.

'Tassy? Have I done something to upset you?'

'Apart from buying my home without having the courtesy to tell me?' she said bitterly.

He sighed. 'Tassy, it wasn't like that.'

'No? How was it, then? Did the agent just imagine your interest?'

'Of course not,' he said shortly. 'I went and saw him on Saturday morning. It was just an idea. I had to sign a revised copy of the tenancy agreement, and while I was in there it occurred to me, and I mentioned it to him. There was no great secret—I just asked if it was likely to come on the market, and he said he'd ask. When I came home there were other things on my mind, if you remember,' he said with irony.

She nodded, ashamed of her lack of trust. 'I'm sorry,' she mumbled. 'I should have known you wouldn't be devious, but I don't have a huge repertoire of experience to call on when it comes to judging character.'

He laughed sadly. 'You and me both. I thought I was getting better, though. I thought you really did care about me, but maybe you were just bored with virginity and decided since I was handy I'd do to relieve you of it—'

'Ben, that's not true!' she exclaimed.

'So why did you decide to change the habits of a lifetime, and why with me?'

She lifted her shoulders in defeat. 'I didn't really decide. It just happened.'

'And now you regret it,' he said flatly.

'No!' she whispered.

'No?'

'No,' she repeated, more firmly. 'No, Ben, I don't. It was wonderful.'

'Why do I hear a but?' he murmured.

Tassy dropped the last little shred of grass and met his eyes reluctantly. 'I just think it was too much, too soon. I don't think I was ready for it.'

'For what it's worth, I didn't exactly plan it that way myself. I don't make a habit of sleeping with women I hardly know. Apart from you and Carla, there's only been one other woman in my life and that was years ago when I was a student.' He stared at his fingers. 'I seem to have this tendency to make long-term commitments to women who don't want to know about for ever.'

So much for the 'hundreds of women' theory—unless he was lying, and she really didn't think he was. 'And you want for ever?' she asked gently.

'Of course I do. I thought everyone did, but apparently I was wrong. I suppose it's possible that one day I'll ask someone to marry me and she'll say yes, but I'm not going to hold my breath. For some reason I seem to be good enough to mow the lawn and put out the rubbish, but not good enough to commit to.'

Tassy felt the pain behind his words, and was about to say something when he got to his feet and chucked the dregs of his tea over the lawn. 'Better get on. I've got some paperwork to catch up on before my clinic.'

He disappeared back over the fence and into his house before she could blink, and she got slowly to her feet, closed the doors and locked them and then stood there for a minute, shocked. Thank God he'd got up, she thought with a hysterical laugh. She'd been about to offer to marry him, just to take away that sadness in his voice!

Her, offer to marry someone? Was she completely round the bend? Her mind, running on ahead, conjured up an image of the house opened back up into one, with little fair-haired moppets with brilliant green eyes running about in the garden in bare feet, and Ben standing behind her with his hands resting on the swollen curve of her pregnant abdomen—

Her hand flew to the flat bowl of her pelvis and hovered there. Had they made a baby this weekend? Was there just such a pretty little moppet in the making?

Pain stabbed through her. It was such a wonderful image, such a glorious, unashamedly romantic and impractical image, but she knew it was false.

Men didn't marry her for love, just for convenience. If she was pregnant she'd have to keep it a secret from him for as long as possible, otherwise she'd have no way of knowing how he really felt. She'd have to give him time to get bored—not that it would take long. What on earth made her think she had what it would take to hold him? Anyway, it was probably all acting, just piling on the angst so that she'd feel sorry for him and let him back into her bed. He'd be bored in no time flat.

Was she just a hardened old cynic?

Or a frustrated romantic afraid to show her true colours?

Or were they one and the same thing...?

'Ben, I can hear a baby crying.'

He laughed. 'Tassy, this is a ward full of hot, fed-up, unhappy children. Most of them are having the odd whinge. Why should one more baby make a difference?'

She shook her head. 'But it's not on the ward. It's outside somewhere, and I can't work out where but it's been crying for absolutely ages and it sounds distressed. It's getting weaker.'

That got his attention. 'How long is ages?'

'An hour, maybe?'

'An hour? You're sure it's the same baby?'

She gave him a dirty look and he threw up his hands.

'Sorry. Of course you can tell—it's your job. Right, we need to find it and make sure it's all right. It's probably just got wind.'

It seemed to be coming from outside so they went out into the corridor and listened, and after a few seconds they looked at each other in puzzlement. 'It's coming from the car park,' Tassy said.

'In this heat? Who in their right mind would leave a baby in a car in this heat? It's scorching hot already!'

Tassy didn't wait to consider what kind of person would do such a thing. She pushed past him, opened the fire door and went out into the car park outside. Following the noise, they tracked the baby down quickly, and as they peered through the window Ben swore softly and with some feeling.

The baby was only a few months old, lying flat on its back in a carrycot in an all-in-one suit, puce to the gills, with the sun full on it and the smallest amount of ventilation from the tilted sunroof. Tassy put her hand inside the sunroof and yelped as her arm touched the metal roof. The baby was hardly crying any longer, just whimpering every now and again, and Tassy could see why.

'The roof's scorching—Ben, it's like an oven in there! We have to get it out!'

He tried the doors, then turned to her and told her to call Security. 'I'm going to smash the window and take the baby into the ward. Go and run a bath of tepid water and we'll get it cooled off and sorted out. Thank God you said something.'

She ran, called Security and went back to the car just as there was a smashing sound. Then Ben appeared with the baby cradled against his shoulder, one huge hand engulfing its head and the other hand under its bottom, and Tassy could see it was hanging limply against him.

Oh, dear God, don't let them have been too late—

He hurried towards her. 'Did you call them?'

'Yes. They were about to come and tell us about the baby anyway, because the car-park attendant was getting a bit concerned.'

'I should damn well hope so,' Ben muttered, and carried the baby past her and into the ward. Anna was running a sink of cool water in the treatment room, and they stripped the baby off and lowered him into the water, splashing it to cool the hot, dry limbs.

'He's dehydrated—must have sweated buckets in that hothouse. What's his temperature, Tassy?'

She checked the gauge. 'Just over forty degrees.'

'Poor little sod,' Ben murmured lovingly, his big hands supporting the baby while Tassy splashed it with the cool water and blew gently over his skin. 'Anna, could you find a fan, please?'

'Sure.' Anna disappeared and came back a moment later with a portable electric fan and set it up so it blew a stream of cool air over the baby.

Ben threw her a distracted smile. 'Thanks. We need to get some fluids into him—I don't know if we'll get a vein and I don't like doing it without parental consent, but frankly I think those parents have forfeited the right to make decisions for their child. I shall make damn sure they're prosecuted for this.'

'You don't know why he was there, Ben. Perhaps they're visiting a very sick relative—maybe dying. You have to know the full story.'

He glared at Tassy. 'No, I don't. This little boy was dying out there. Ten minutes more and he would have been a goner. I don't have to know anything else apart from that. Check his temperature again.'

She did, and it was down a fraction. 'Will he drink, do you suppose?' she asked Ben.

Ben joggled the baby, and he stirred slightly, whimpering again.

'He's not unconscious—we could try just a little saline. That won't do his lungs any harm if he does inhale it.'

She got some cool sterile saline solution from a sachet of IV fluid, and offered it to the baby cautiously. The effect was miraculous. He started drinking immediately, and it seemed to revive him.

'Not too much at once,' Ben warned. 'We don't want to start him vomiting. Give him some more in a couple of minutes.'

She put the bottle down and splashed his front, while Ben dipped the little boy in and out of the water to cool his back. Finally, after nearly an hour of fanning and splashing and sipping, his temperature was down to thirty-eight degrees and Ben felt happy to stop.

'We'll wrap him in a wet sheet and fan him—keep the sheet wet and monitor him constantly. We don't want him going too low, either, and because he's so young he's likely to have problems with temperature regulation for a little while now. We might need to send him up to SCBU if he doesn't remain stable.'

'I'll put Anna on to special him—I wonder when the

parents will turn up?' Tassy said, lifting the little baby out of Ben's hands and lying him on the wet sheet she had prepared. Just then a nurse stuck her head round the door of the treatment room.

'That baby you rescued from the car park—was it a boy, about four months old, dressed in a white and yellow all-in-one?'

Ben's mouth flattened to a grim line. 'It was—why?'

'They've got Mum in A and E—she came to return some crutches and left the baby in the car, then someone knocked her down in the car park. She's been stressing about a baby, but they've only just been able to make sense of it. They've been looking for a baby in the hospital—Security put two and two together, apparently. How's it doing?'

'Tell her he's fine,' Ben said. 'Ask if we can treat as necessary—get a consent form down there and get it filled in. We'd better have some details as well.' He turned to Tassy. 'Can you spare her for a minute?'

She nodded. 'Yes, of course. Once we've got all the info we can sort him out a bit better.' She smiled at Ben. 'And I will resist the urge to say "I told you so" about hearing the full story—'

She dodged his mock punch, and returned the grin. 'At least she wasn't ill-treating him, and it looks like we'll have a happy ending.'

'But only because of your persistence. Well done, Tassy.'

His quiet words of praise meant more to her than they had any business meaning, and because of that she was a little short.

'Anybody would have done it. It just happened to be me—'

'I know, but credit where it's due. It was you, and you did well. You should be proud of yourself. I am.'

And with that he walked off, leaving her hot and bothered and grinning like a Cheshire cat.

'About that meal I promised you.'

Tassy looked up at Ben and wondered if she'd ever be able to do it without her heart doing stupid acrobatics. 'What meal is that?'

He grinned. 'The one you're definitely maybe going to let me take you for.'

'Oh—that one,' she said casually, stifling the grin. 'What of it?'

He propped himself on the edge of the desk in front of her so that she was acutely aware of the way his trousers pulled taut over his lean hips. 'How about tonight?'

'Tonight?' she squeaked, and cleared her throat. 'Tonight I'm—ah—doing something else.'

'Such as?'

'Sorting out my tiddlywinks?'

He snorted. 'Is that yes or no?'

She stopped prevaricating and turned to face him, then immediately regretted it because those gorgeous green eyes caressed her and left her feeling weak-kneed and silly again. 'Ben, this is all happening too fast,' she protested softly.

'Just a meal,' he said, his hands coming up to cup her shoulders and ease her closer.

'And pigs fly,' she retorted, pushing his hands aside. 'I know what you want.'

'I didn't notice you protesting too much at the weekend,' he reminded her with a teasing smile. 'And I really did mean just a meal. Anything else is up to you. We'll play it entirely your way.'

She eyed him sceptically. 'Can I trust you?'

He laughed. 'I think so. One well-aimed kick should settle me down if not.'

'Just a meal?'

'Just a meal.'

'Chinese?'

He grimaced. 'If you like. I was going to take you to an Italian restaurant, but whatever you fancy.'

'And no hanky-panky?'

The laughter died in his eyes. 'Tassy, I promise you, we'll do whatever you want.'

She turned away, wondering if she could cope with the temptation of Ben's company or if all that proximity would nobble her resolve all over again.

'OK,' she said finally. 'Chinese—nothing too elaborate. This is just a simple meal.'

'If you insist.'

'I do.'

'Fine. I'll book a table for eight o'clock.'

And he walked off again, leaving her cursing the stupid impulse that had made her give in to his persuasion.

'Dr Lazaar says I can go home soon—maybe another couple of weeks.'

Tassy grinned at Sam. 'I know. Good news, isn't it? You're much better now, aren't you?'

He nodded. 'Much. I'm not twitching about any more, and I don't hurt so much now. That's cool. Have you seen today's tie?'

It was another cartoon tie, the fourteenth different one

she'd seen him in, or thereabouts. He must spend a fortune on ties. She smiled at Sam. 'Yes, I've seen it.'

'I'm going to ask my Mum to find him a tie as a thank-you present when I go home—something really gross. He'll like that.'

Tassy laughed. 'I'm sure he will,' she agreed. She checked that Sam was comfortable and had enough to keep him amused and then went to see how Andrew Harvey and Nicky Coulter were doing. The answer was fairly well, although they were both still feeling pretty rough and were not yet eating.

The mothers seemed to have instituted some uneasy truce and Tassy noticed that, although the boys ignored each other while their mothers were there, the second their backs were turned they were signing to each other and giggling. The content of their conversation was innocent enough, too, she knew, having eavesdropped, as it were, with her eyes, and she just wished Mrs Harvey would relent and allow their friendship—even supervise it, if need be, and allow Nicky into their home.

All the boy needed was a friend, and if they were adequately supervised Tassy didn't see how it could do any harm, but, then, she wasn't a mother.

At least, not yet. She wondered again if their precipitate behaviour would have any aftereffects, and found herself drawn towards the cot that contained Paul Reed, the baby from the car park. He was stable at thirty-seven degrees, now dressed in normal light clothes and maintaining his body temperature at the correct level without any apparent difficulty. He would be able to go home the next day. He had been lucky, she realised, and wondered if Ben was right and he did owe her his life.

It was a chilling and a heart-warming thought all at

once. With one last lingering look at the sleeping baby, she took off her tabard, handed over the ward to her staff nurse and then left to get ready for her date.

My God, she thought, a date! I haven't had a date in years, not a real one, and certainly not one with a certifiable hunk like Ben! It was strange, but even after all they'd shared over the weekend she felt as if it was a milestone in their relationship, and she was almost paralysed with nerves by the time he knocked on her door at seven-thirty.

Closing her eyes and drawing in a huge deep breath, she forced herself to relax and opened the door.

He looked wonderful—and he was wearing a conventional dark suit, a white shirt and, most amazing of all, a dark red Paisley tie.

'What?' she teased, flicking the tie with her finger. 'No rabbits?'

He grinned. 'You haven't seen the boxer shorts yet.'

'No, and I'm not going to, remember?' she said squashingly.

He wasn't squashed. He just grinned even wider and ran his eyes over her. 'You look lovely, Tassy. That dress really suits you.'

She felt the soft colour flood her cheeks and fumbled in her handbag for a moment to cover her confusion. It didn't work because when she looked up he was watching her with patient understanding, and his smile was gentle and too knowing. 'Shall we go?' he said, and she was only too ready to get in the car where he would have to concentrate on the road instead of her.

Not that she really minded his reaction, of course. She'd dressed with considerable care and if he hadn't noticed she would have been disappointed. She was just shy, strange though it was after all they'd shared, and the short drive to the restaurant gave her time to recover her composure.

The meal was wonderful—nothing overdone, and he didn't go mad and order everything on the menu to impress her as Derek would have done when he was trying to sweet-talk her into marriage. They shared half a bottle of wine, and because he was driving Ben only had one small glass so Tassy ended up drinking the rest.

'Are you trying to get me tiddly?' she asked him jokingly as he drained the bottle into her glass.

He grinned. 'No. I would have ordered a whole bottle if I had been. Have some more sizzling prawns.'

She shook her head. 'Honestly, I couldn't eat another scrap. You finish them.'

He shrugged, scraped the dish onto his plate and added the rest of the special fried rice, then polished off the lot.

'You're slick with those chopsticks, aren't you?' she observed, watching him.

'Have to be—this is my only decent tie. You never know when I might need it next for a wedding or a funeral.'

She didn't believe it for a moment. Anyone who had fourteen cartoon ties had more than one ordinary one. 'How did you get started on the crazy ties, anyway?' she asked.

'Oh, them. My mother bought me the first one when I did my first spot of paediatrics. She thought I ought to present a less threatening image, and as I'm so big the only thing to do was make me into a friendly giant.'

'So she bought you a cute tie.'

He laughed. 'Actually, it was ghastly, but the kids

seemed to like it and it gave me the idea. Since then I've just sort of collected them. If I see one in a shop I buy it, and people who know me well enough often get me one for birthdays and Christmas, that kind of thing. It's become my trademark.'

'Sam really looks forward to seeing you every day, you know.'

Ben grinned. 'He's a good kid. I'm glad he's getting better without any complications.'

'The baby looks stable, too.'

'Yes. I popped in before I came home—I just missed you. You'd left a few minutes before. He's a lovely little chap.'

'And his mother was innocent.'

He gave a rueful grin. 'Yes, I'm sorry, you were right, but people can be so foul it doesn't come easily any longer, giving them the benefit of the doubt.'

Tassy couldn't argue with that. It was, after all, the principle she was using to judge Ben. She felt a pang of guilt and suppressed it. So what if she felt unsure of him? It was, after all, only just over two weeks since they'd met, far too soon to know anyone well enough to be sure you could trust them—and just because she wanted to didn't mean she could.

She scraped up a smile. 'I'll forgive you for being a cynic,' she told him.

'So you can be one too?'

He saw too much. She looked away, fiddling with the last scraps of rice in her bowl, and she heard him give a quiet sigh.

'Fancy coffee?'

She shook her head. 'Not really. I'd be quite happy to go home—it's been a long day.'

He called for the bill, ushered her out and drove her home, walking her to her door.

'I don't suppose there's any point in asking you in for coffee?' he suggested, and she shook her head.

'I'm sorry, Ben.'

His smile was wry and understanding. 'That's OK. I promised we'd play it your way.' He took her shoulders in his hands, bent his head and kissed her lightly on the lips.

Before she was ready to let him go he lifted his head, stepped back and turned on his heel, striding briskly across the front lawn and in through his door. It closed with a click that seemed to echo through the night and reverberate around her empty, lonely heart...

CHAPTER SEVEN

IT WAS an odd week. Nothing out of the ordinary happened on Tuesday, but on Wednesday they heard that the GP who had been responsible for poor little Heidi had never qualified.

'His father was a GP, apparently, but he was kicked out of medical school for terminal incompetence,' Ben told her. 'He never finished his course, but obviously he'd acquired enough info along the way to be convincing.'

'What about his certificates? References, that sort of thing?'

'Invented. Fabricated—the whole lot of them. The practice was pushed, they took him on in good faith after a couple of quick phone calls. He's done it before, apparently, each time using a different name. They've arrested him and he's singing like a canary, so the police told me. They want us to testify, of course.'

'Of course. So how long was he working there?'

'Two months.'

'And none of his colleagues smelled a rat?' Tassy snorted. 'Were they all asleep?'

'Just pushed.' Ben shrugged. 'My father's a GP. I understand how it could happen. There just isn't time to watch your colleagues. It's hard enough to get through your own work.'

'Tell me about it,' Tassy said with feeling. The day was running away with her. There were children coming

in for surgery the following day, a list going on at the
moment with children going back and forth from Theatre
all morning, a fight breaking out by the sound of it down
at the orthopaedic end—

'Ben, I have to go. I'll see you later.'

She marched down to the far end of the ward, broke
up the pillow fight and paused by the two lads with
salmonella poisoning. 'How are you feeling?' she said
and signed.

'Better,' Nicky told her. Andrew made a 'so-so' gesture with his hand. There was no sign of the mums so
she perched on the edge of Nicky's bed where Andrew
could see her easily and asked what had actually happened.

'Mum bought some chicken stuff in sauce home from
the club, but she forgot to put it in the fridge. When
Andrew came round the next evening we heated it up a
bit and ate it, but I suppose it had been hanging round
and stuff—anyway, it was pretty gross so we didn't eat
a lot.'

'And your mother didn't know you were there?' she
signed to Andrew.

He shook his head and dragged his finger across his
throat.

'So how does she think you both got ill?
Coincidence?'

They shrugged, and Tassy sighed. 'I think you should
tell them.'

Andrew started waving his arms about and signing
like mad, and Nicky babbled frantically, 'But then
Mum'll get in trouble for bringing the food home and
she'd lose her job, and then we'll have to move out—'

'Hey, hey, hang on,' Tassy said, stopping them in

their tracks. 'I'm sure the food was all right when it left the club, or there would have been a big outbreak by now. It must have gone off sitting in the kitchen for twenty-four hours. How hot does it get in your kitchen?'

'Very—and the worktop's right in the sun,' Nicky told her.

'So, if the food went off at home, it's not a problem where it came from. Most chicken and egg products contain the salmonella germ. We just have to make sure we cook them very thoroughly, don't let them hang around in a warm place and eat them as fresh as possible. I still think that your mothers should know you were together because they have a right to know.'

'My mum knows,' Nicky told her. 'It's Andrew's mum that will kick up such a fuss.'

'Kick up such a fuss about what?' Mrs Harvey said from behind Tassy.

Andrew, seeing her, slid down into the bed and groaned, and Nicky went bright red and looked away.

'They have something to tell you,' Tassy informed the woman. 'Please listen and try not to be angry.'

And she went away and left them all to it. She felt a bit mean, but she thought it was high time that the boys opened up and admitted how much time they'd been spending together. After all, from what Tassy could gather, they weren't out stealing cars or shoplifting—they were just two lonely boys who each needed a friend.

She didn't have time to check on how the confession had gone until much later, and she was amazed when she went down the ward to find both mothers together, deep in conversation. She arched a brow at Andrew and he winked, and she let out the mental breath she had been holding since that morning and winked back.

She didn't know how they'd done it, but they seemed to have bridged the gulf between the two families. A little while later Ben came round and examined the boys, and declared Nicky to be ready to go home. 'I think I'd like Andrew to stay in for another day, if possible, just to get him onto solids and keeping them down before we discharge him.'

'Can't I stay with him?' Nicky pleaded. 'I still feel sick when I eat.'

Ben gave him a considering look, clearly not taken in by the faked symptoms and sudden listlessness of the boy, but to Tassy's surprise he nodded. 'All right, you are looking a bit peaky. We'll send you both home to-morrow morning if you're better.'

Nicky punched the air victoriously and then collapsed back onto the bed with a staged groan. Ben, barely suppressing a smile, nodded at the mothers and looked at Tassy.

'Have you got a minute, Sister?' he asked.

Not ward business, I'll warrant, she thought to herself, but she went anyway. Sucker that she was, she was quite happy to be in his company.

'Not a lot wrong with him,' Ben murmured as they walked up the ward together.

'Not a lot, no, but he will keep Andrew company and that's difficult as he's deaf.' She shot him a sideways look. 'So, what did you want to talk to me about? It's a bit busy round here today.'

'I had noticed. I'm going to take the dogs for a walk after work—I wondered if you wanted to join me?'

'The dogs?'

'Bill and Ben.'

She smiled. 'And who are you—Little Weed?'

'Hardly.' He chuckled. 'I think that's Mrs Gates—she's apparently feeble, but she keeps those two dogs in order.'

Tassy laughed. 'Well, mostly.'

'Mostly. Anyway, I'm trying to ask you if you'd like to join us, but you keep changing the subject.'

She shrugged. 'Yeah, sure, I'll go for a walk. What time?'

'About six-thirty? Should be cooler then. We can take a picnic.'

'A picnic?'

'Yes—sandwiches, fruit—nothing elaborate. I might even have a quiche in the fridge so we wouldn't even have to make sandwiches. What do you say?'

'Seems rather a lot of fuss for a stroll along the river.'

'Ah, well, I thought we could go somewhere in the car and find a nice walk—some woods or something, a bit of heathland.'

'It's turning into an expedition. Are you sure you aren't taking a Primus stove and sleeping bag?'

Something wicked twinkled in the back of his eyes. 'It could be arranged—sleeping out under the stars with the woman of my dreams—'

'In your dreams, Ben, that's all it would be. OK, I'll come for a walk—but just a walk.'

'And a picnic?'

'A bit of quiche and an apple.'

'Done.' He grinned, waggled his fingers at her and strode off, leaving her to catch up with the waiting mountain of paperwork.

Mrs Harvey came and interrupted her just as she was

getting stuck in. 'Sister?' she said hesitantly from the doorway.

Tassy sighed inwardly and dredged up a smile. 'Come in, Mrs Harvey. What can I do for you?'

She perched on the edge of a chair and twisted her fingers together. 'I just wanted to thank you for making the boys be honest. I've tried so hard to drum honesty into Andrew, but he's been acting so oddly recently. Now I know why, of course. He and Nicky have been seeing each other almost every day, but because I didn't approve he was having to lie to me. It's really made him miserable because he is basically very honest.

'Anyway, I've had a chat with Nicky's mother, Lyn, and, well, I was surprised what a nice woman she is. Do you know, Nicky's father used to knock them about? How dreadful to be trapped with a man like that, and then they want her to say who he is so they can get money off him for maintenance for Nicky, but she's terrified he'll come after them and, from what she's said, I wouldn't be surprised.'

She shook her head. 'I'm so lucky with Nigel—he looks after us all so well. I'd hate to have to go and work in that seedy place. Lyn says the men all try it on—well, anyway, I just wanted to thank you for making them tell the truth.'

'I'm sure the boys' friendship is quite innocent, Mrs Harvey,' Tassy felt compelled to say. 'I know it's none of my business, but Nicky seems a nice kid, and I'm sure he wouldn't lead Andrew astray.'

Mrs Harvey coloured a little, perhaps remembering her earlier condemnation of the family, and admitted she'd told Lyn that Nicky was welcome to come round any time he wanted to. 'I'd rather keep an eye on them than have them unsupervised at the Coulters' flat, but I don't see why the boys shouldn't spend time together. Andrew does get lonely and he can't just watch the television like other boys. Anyway, must get on.'

Tassy watched her go and shook her head. Another happy ending? It seemed to be so easy to arrange other people's lives. If only she could sort her own out so well.

She glanced at the calendar and chewed her lip. Her next period was due this weekend so it was extremely unlikely that she would be pregnant, but she was now kicking herself for not going straight to the doctor and getting a morning-after prescription. There was some crazy part of her that cherished the idea of a baby that had held her back, and now it was too late. Oh, well, only a few more days to wait and she'd know for sure.

And if she didn't get this paperwork done she'd be unemployed as well as pregnant...

'I thought you'd bottled out.'

She shut her car door and went over to Ben's car. He was folding down the back seat and loading in a coolbox, and she eyed it sceptically.

'Quiche and an apple?'

'Of course. Don't want it hot, do you?' he said with a quick grin. He glanced at his watch. 'Go on, then, you've got three minutes to change and get out here or I'm coming in to fetch you.'

'Yes, sir,' she said drily, and went. She did hurry—not because of his threat but just because after the hectic and tedious day she'd had the thought of walking the dogs through shady woodland and sharing a picnic with Ben was absolutely wonderful.

So she flung off her uniform, pulled on jeans and a

T-shirt, snagged up a sweatshirt in case it was cool later
and ran downstairs, trainers in hand, just as he tapped
on the door.

'Come in,' she yelled, and he leant in and grinned.
'Attagirl. Let's be having you, then.'

She went barefoot and put her shoes on in the car,
and they picked up the dogs *en route* and loaded them
into the back.

'You can manage, can't you?' Mrs Gates agitated.
'Only Ben can be so naughty—Bill's never given me a
moment's worry, but Ben, well, I think some dogs are
just naturally wicked.'

'I'm sure we'll cope, won't we, boys?' Ben said. His
namesake grinned from the back of the car, looking as
if butter wouldn't melt in his mouth, and with another
assurance to Mrs Gates they set off.

'I've found a place on the map. It's quite a way but
someone said it was a lovely walk. Here—can you navi-
gate?'

He handed her the map, pointed out the spot they were
heading to and settled back against the seat with a sigh.
'What a day—did you get the boys sorted out?'

She laughed. 'Mrs Harvey now feels sorry for them
all and is taking them under her wing, I think. Talk about
going from the sublime to the ridiculous. I'm pleased for
the boys, but I think she's a real fuss-pot.'

'Maybe one day when we've got children we'll understand,' Ben said, and although she knew he didn't mean
'we' as in them together, mutually as it were, just the
sound of the words was enough to trigger that silly pipe
dream again—

'Damn. You should have turned off there.'

He slowed down, turned round and went back, then shot her a grin. 'Try and stay awake, eh, pet?'

'Don't "eh, pet" me. I was distracted. Anyway, I don't know the road any more than you do. I've never been out here before.'

'All the more reason why you need to concentrate—and, on the subject of being distracted, could you try and persuade this dog not to lick the back of my neck?'

Tassy turned round and saw Ben—of course—lying down behind the driver's seat with his chin resting on the back of the seat and his long, pink tongue snaking out and wrapping round Ben's neck under the headrest.

'Hey, horrid dog, that's disgusting. Leave him alone,' she commanded, and Ben grinned and lolled his tongue and rolled over, looking cute. She laughed and turned back. 'Hopeless. He's a waste of a good skin.'

Ben chuckled. 'Just so long as he gets attached to us and doesn't run off so we have to go home without him. I don't fancy going back to Mrs Gates with just Bill.'

Tassy shuddered. 'No. I don't think she'd ever get over it.'

'He'd turn up. He's tagged—someone would hand him over to the police. It will just waste the entire night if we have to stand around calling him.'

'We could always keep him on the lead,' Tassy suggested.

Ben snorted. 'OK. You can take him. He'll pull all the way.'

'It's better than chasing him all night.'

However, when they arrived Ben the dog pre-empted their sensible decision by leaping out of the car and running off, nose to the ground, in search of some elusive scent. Bill followed more slowly, and with a resigned shrug Ben picked up the redundant leads, locked the car and set off after them with Tassy.

'What about the picnic?' she said.

'I thought we'd come back for it, unless you're starving?'

She shook her head. It had been too hot and busy a day to get hungry. 'Later will be fine,' she agreed, and scanned the heathland ahead of them for the dogs. 'I wonder if there's any danger of being able to catch them?' she mused.

'Dunno. Let's find out.' He gave a piercing whistle, called the dogs' names and stared in disbelief as they ran back immediately.

'Good grief,' Tassy said faintly. 'That's amazing.'

'The voice of authority,' Ben said with a stunned laugh. 'OK, boys, off you go.'

They had a wonderful walk. The dogs sniffed all manner of enticing smells, and Tassy found her hand commandeered by Ben as he helped her over a stile. For some reason he held onto it and she let him so that they ended up strolling along under the trees hand in hand.

It slowed their pace, but they didn't care and the dogs seemed happy enough in the undergrowth. They passed another couple similarly occupied, and after they'd gone past Ben released her hand and draped his arm round her shoulder, pulling her up against his side so that she felt the hard nudge of his hipbone against hers as they walked.

It stirred memories of the weekend—memories she was trying very hard to banish, but failing miserably. She ached to turn into his arms, but she knew it would be foolish. They had to spend some time getting to know each other—weeks, probably months—before they could make any kind of commitment.

To allow the physical side of their relationship to develop unchecked until then was crazy, she told herself—over and over and over again.

They got back to the car after an hour or more of this torture, and Ben carried the cool-box from the car to the picnic benches set up under the trees and pulled out the contents.

'Quiche and apples?' she said again.

'There is quiche, and some apples.'

'And melon, and sandwiches—is that smoked salmon in them?'

He grinned. 'I had a little time on my hands.'

'And wine—you're trying to get me drunk again!'

He laughed. 'It's not wine, it's grape juice.'

'And cream cakes!' she said with a little shriek. 'Ben, I can't eat cream cakes, I'll be huge!'

'Fiddlesticks. You're gorgeous. Anyway, it's mostly fruit. Here, have a plate.'

She took a plate and allowed him to pile a few things on it, then snatched it away before he overdid it. She watched him eat, though, marvelling at his appetite, although of course he did have a big frame to cart round with him.

Not that she was exactly skimpy in the frame department, but she certainly wasn't as heavy as him by miles. She remembered the feel of his leg flung over hers, all that muscle pinning her down, and a little moan sneaked out of her throat before she could trap it.

'That good?' he said with a laugh.

'I'm hungrier than I thought,' she lied to cover herself,

and then for her sins had to eat another handful of goodies he dropped on her plate.

He stretched and then dropped his elbows to the table and leant on it, looking out over her shoulder at the view behind her. 'It's gorgeous here,' he murmured. 'What a lovely evening.'

His eyes flicked to hers, fixing on them with gentle intensity. 'I haven't had so much fun in ages,' he confessed.

'Fun? We just walked the dogs,' she said with an edgy laugh.

'That's what I mean. Just walking the dogs sounds so easy, but if you haven't got a dog it's a little tricky. It's also having someone to walk the dog with—or even just to go for a stroll with on your own. It's hard to walk hand in hand with yourself.'

Tassy looked down at her plate, still piled with food. 'Don't make something out of it that wasn't there, Ben,' she said quietly.

'But it was there.'

'No.'

'Yes.' He took her hand. 'Yes, Tassy, it was. It is.'

She pulled her hand back and stood up. 'We ought to be going, it's late. Dogs, here!'

They were there in a second, lured by the promise of food, and she took them to the car and put them in, before giving them her leftovers. They even had the grace to lick up the crumbs so he had nothing to complain about.

They didn't talk much on the way back. Tassy knew she'd spoilt their evening, but it was Ben's fault. He'd pushed too hard, and she'd had no choice.

Still, at least they hadn't lost either of the dogs. They

took them back, returned them to Mrs Gates and Tassy sat in the car and listened as Ben made arrangements to pick them up on Saturday and deliver them to his parents. Mrs Gates was due to go into hospital on Sunday morning for her operation on Monday, and Tassy promised to water the garden and keep an eye on the place for her.

When they arrived back at the cottage she was out of the car and heading for her door before he had switched off the engine. He followed her, catching up with her just as the door swung open.

'May I come in?'

'Only if you promise not to touch me.'

His eyes were filled with reproach as he looked at her. 'Tassy, I'm not going to hurt you,' he murmured.

She snorted. There was more than one way of being hurt, and she was well on the way to it already.

'Come outside with me and sit in the garden and have a glass of wine,' he coaxed. 'And, no, I'm not trying to get you drunk, or seduce you.'

She hesitated for an age, and then with a ragged sigh she gave in. 'OK,' she agreed, 'just for a little while—and just one glass.'

He smiled and grazed her cheek with his knuckles. 'See you in the garden,' he said cheerily, and turned and went out, closing the door softly behind him.

She sat down abruptly on the sofa and rested her head on her knees. What was she thinking about? Spending all this time with him was crazy!

But you can't get to know him if you don't spend time with him, her alter ego was wheedling. She ignored it. She wasn't in the least bit ready to listen to that sort of advice.

She went upstairs and combed her hair, then the alter ego interfered again and puffed a little drift of light summery scent over her throat. 'Idiot,' she mumbled, put the lipstick down before she could be silly and went down to Ben's garden.

She smelt wonderful. He was going to die if he had to keep his hands to himself much longer, but he was going to die if he didn't, he was sure of that. Tassy would take care of it.

She was holding her glass in front of her like a shield and glaring at him almost defiantly over it, as if daring him to get her drunk and have his evil way with her.

The idea had merit. It seemed a hell of a long time since he'd held her in his arms that weekend, and if she thought that one short night was enough to slake his need for her she was in for a shock—similarly, if she imagined he was going to give up and lie down as easily as all that.

He'd been waiting for her all his life, and there was no way he was going to allow her to brush him aside like a troublesome fly. God, he loved her. Every move, every look, every touch was torment. He could quite see why men went off and joined the foreign legion when their womenfolk were unfaithful. The very thought of Tassy with anyone else was enough to send him into a murderous rage.

But this—lying here in the garden in the swinging hammock he'd bought the other day while Tassy sat near him on a sun lounger and sipped her wine suspiciously—this was bliss. The evening was cool, the sun setting far over to the north-west and streaking the sky with purple and gold and scarlet, and the sounds and scents of the country were all around him. What more could he want?

Tassy on the hammock with him, their limbs entangled—oh, hell, he was going to embarrass himself in a minute. He shifted uncomfortably in his jeans and tried to think about something mundane, but he failed.

He gave up and watched her instead, and wondered if he had enough self-control to keep spending time with her like this without jumping her bones like a randy adolescent.

'It was a nice place, that forest, wasn't it?' he said to break the silence.

'Lovely. I enjoyed it, thank you.'

Damn, why did she sound so formal? He turned on his side so he could see her better. 'This is idyllic. Sunset, cool breeze, chilled wine, the sounds of evening, the company of a beautiful woman—'

'Ben,' she said warningly, a little scowl marring her features.

He threw up his hands and laughed. 'Sorry. Just an observation.'

'Well, you aren't very observant.'

He tutted. 'You fishing again, young woman?'

'Don't be ridiculous,' she snapped. 'Ben, you promised—'

'I know. I'm sorry.' He rolled onto his back again and stared up at the darkening sky. The stars were starting to show, bright pinpricks in the velvet night, and he wished she were lying there beside him instead of sitting four feet away and glowering.

'All we need now to complete the scene is nappies on the line and the dogs at our feet,' he said lazily, and knew at once it was the wrong thing to have said.

'How domesticated,' she replied, her voice tight. 'Roses round the door, two point four kids, black Labradors——'

'Golden retrievers, actually.'

'You know what I mean. It's idealistic nonsense, Ben. Real people don't live like that.'

'My parents do. My sister does. They're real people. I think it sounds wonderful.'

'It's a dream, Ben,' she said, and there seemed to him to be a note of desperation in her voice. 'Just a dream.'

'It could be real, Tassy,' he said softly. 'It could be real, and it could be ours. I don't suppose you'd like to join me and we could dream it together?'

Their eyes locked, and for an age she sat there staring at him longingly. Then she put her glass down and stood up, and he knew she was going to run away again.

He tried to get up, but the hammock took its revenge and dumped him on the floor. By the time he'd got to his feet she'd gone, slipping away into the night like a wraith.

Fanciful nonsense. She'd just walked off. He heard the defiant little click of her French doors as he straightened up, and with a muttered curse he picked up her glass and drained it, then topped it up again. His own was broken—he knew that because he'd knelt on it as he'd fallen out of the hammock.

He went inside, peeled off his jeans and glared sourly at the neat slice across his knee. Damn. It would need stitches. He contemplated asking Tassy to drive him to the hospital, and thought better of it. Pulling out his sewing kit, he threaded a needle, dipped it in whisky and pushed it into the skin.

'Ow—damn.' He dropped the needle back into the

box and glared at his leg. Sticking plaster wouldn't be strong enough to hold it, not right across his knee like that.

He buried his pride, went round to her front door and tapped on it. 'Tassy? I've got a problem,' he told her.

She opened the door, took one look at him in his boxer shorts and T-shirt and went to shut the door again.

He jammed his foot in it—his bare foot—just in time to stop it closing. It made him wince, but he shouldered the door open and went in. 'I'm not after your precious bloody virtue,' he growled, irritated now. 'I've cut my knee—it needs stitches.'

She blinked at him and looked at his knee, and said, 'Ouch. How did you do that?'

'I fell on my glass,' he muttered crossly, wondering how long she was going to torture him with stupid questions.

'Want me to take you in?'

'No, I want you to sew it up with rafia—of course I want you to take me in.'

She folded her arms and leant against the wall. 'Then I suggest you ask nicely,' she said in a prim little voice, as if it hadn't been her fault in the first place that it had happened.

He ground his teeth and dredged up a smile. 'Please will you take me to A and E for some stitches?'

'No—'

'What?' he yelled.

'I'll take you up to the ward and stitch you myself. It'll be quicker and quieter—but, unless you want to really set the gossips talking, I suggest you put something on over your boxer shorts.'

He looked down at Micky Mouse chasing Minnie all

round the fabric, and sighed. 'I'll see you at the door in a moment.'

It was an hour before they were back, his knee repaired with a neat row of sutures any surgeon would have been proud of. She sat him down, made him put his leg up and gave him a cup of tea. 'You ought to go to bed, really,' she told him.

'Are you offering to tuck me up?' he asked with a lazy grin. He knew what the answer would be, but he couldn't seem to stop himself from making the remark.

She handed him the tea without a word, sat down opposite with hers and sipped it while she looked at his leg. 'I think you should have a day off,' she told him.

'I can't. Too much to do. I'll just have to put it up every now and again, if someone kind will give me tea and sympathy.'

She snorted. 'Tea, yes. Sympathy's a bit thin on the ground at the moment, seeing as it was your own fault.'

'I was only going to kiss you goodnight,' he said reasonably.

'A glass of wine, you said. There was nothing in the contract about a goodnight kiss.'

'It was in the small print. You must have missed it.'

She sighed. 'You never give up, do you?'

He met her eyes. 'Do you really want me to?' he asked seriously.

She looked away after a long, heart-searching moment. 'I don't know,' she murmured.

'Tassy, I meant it, you know. I do love you.'

She got up. He'd got too close to the knuckle again, dammit, he thought, but she came and perched beside him and looked down into his eyes, her own troubled.

'I wish I could believe you,' she said, and then she kissed him goodnight, very gently, a chaste and rather thoughtful kiss, and left him sitting there wondering if there was, after all, hope for them…

CHAPTER EIGHT

TASSY thought she must have been mad, encouraging Ben like that. Fancy kissing him goodnight, even if it was only a peck, but he'd looked so sincere when he'd told her he loved her.

He was hobbling round the ward at the moment, his leg rather stiff and straight, but his grin was undiminished and her ridiculous heart was quite absurdly pleased to have him around.

He tracked her down in the treatment room where she was changing a dressing on a burns patient. 'Can I see you when you've got a minute, Sister?' he said after chatting to their little patient to take his mind off what she was doing.

'Sure. How about tomorrow afternoon?'

'Any time in the next five minutes will do well. I'll be in your office.'

She handed over to Anna to finish off the dressing and followed him out. 'It had better be important,' she said warningly.

He grinned, dispelling any fears that it was. 'What are you doing on Saturday night?'

'Saturday—you interrupted my treatment of a patient to ask me what I'm doing on Saturday night?' she said, her voice rising in a squeak.

'There's a ball—a Midsummer Ball at the town hall, organised by the League of Friends of the hospital. I've managed to track down a couple of tickets—'

'So?'

'So I wondered if you'd do me the honour of joining me.'

She opened her mouth to make a squashing remark but noticed that his eyes were serious, although a smile was still playing around his lips.

'Please?' he added, and she felt herself toppling.

'I've never been to a ball before,' she said softly after an age.

'So here's your chance. You'll love it.'

'What makes you so sure?'

He grinned. 'Because you'll be with me.'

His eyes were still serious, as if her answer really mattered to him, and she thought how lovely it would be to be with him—to be in his arms and dance with him. It would be probably the first time she'd danced with anyone and been able to wear high heels and still look up.

'Can I think about it?' she said, weakening.

The grin faded. 'A straight yes would be awfully nice, instead of yet another maybe.'

She took a slow deep breath, and met his eyes again. 'Thank you. That would be lovely.'

'That's a yes?' he said, sounding faintly shocked.

She smiled. 'That's a yes, Ben,' she confirmed, and then had another thought. 'Will it be frightfully glamorous?'

'Oh, frightfully,' he teased.

She sighed and smacked his arm, suppressing the little bubble of excitement that was fizzing about inside her. 'I'd better go shopping, then, hadn't I? I haven't got a ball gown. I might sneak out at lunchtime if Anna can come with me.' He shifted his weight, and she glanced down at his leg, remorseful because she hadn't even asked about it. 'How is it?' she asked, nodding at the knee he was favouring.

'Stiff. I can't bend it because the stitches pull. I have to warn you, I may only be able to shuffle on Saturday.'

She laughed. 'Good, because that's all I can do, anyway. I must get on—try and rest your leg.'

'Yes, Mum,' he quipped.

'Mum, indeed,' she muttered to herself as she walked away, but the little smile wouldn't go away and she found herself humming as she went about her work.

'You sound happy,' Josh murmured in her ear later as he came up to do a round.

'Me?' She flashed him a smile. 'I'm going to a ball.'

Something flickered in his eyes—concern? Relief? 'With Ben?'

She nodded. 'Yes—on Saturday. Are you and Melissa going?'

'Hope so. I don't know if she'll be feeling up to it—it's only five weeks since she had her hysterectomy. We'll see. We'll probably pop in for a while, just to say we've been. Mind you, she says she feels better now than she has for years, and she certainly looks it. Having the two children so close together was a bit much for her, but the endometriosis didn't give us a whole lot of choice. It was have them quick, or not have them.'

'I'm sure you did the right thing.'

He gave a groan that was half-laugh. 'Maybe when they're older I'll agree with you, but just now they're a bit of a handful at two and half and one and a bit!'

'Well, at least you had one of each so you can't regret your decision on those grounds.'

Josh shook his head. 'I couldn't regret it, anyway.

Both Benedict and Katie are well, and there was no choice about the hysterectomy. Lissa was so ill every time she had a period it would have been madness not to have the op—anyway, it's all over now and she's really relieved, and the kids are great and everything in the garden's rosy.'

He grinned. 'Sorry to sound so disgustingly self-satisfied, but it's difficult not to when everything's going so well.'

Tassy tried to smile, but it didn't really reach her eyes and Josh, of course, being Josh, noticed immediately. 'Ah, Tassy, I'm sorry. That was so thoughtless. I didn't mean to go on and on.'

She gave him a rueful grin. 'That's OK, Josh, we can't all be miserable. I'm glad you're happy—truly.'

Josh hesitated, and then said, 'Tassy, this Ben Lazaar guy—he's not crowding you, is he? Pushing?'

She shook her head. 'Not really. A bit, but nothing I can't handle.'

'You want me to tell him to back off?'

She laughed. 'Josh, what is this—the Mafia?'

His neck coloured and he apologised again, a little stiffly. 'I just thought if he was making a nuisance of himself, well, I could tell him to back off. If you don't want me to, that's fine.'

'He's OK. He's very sweet to me. It might even do me good, if I can cope with it.'

'And if you can't?'

She shrugged slightly. 'Just be there for me, Josh,' she whispered, and then turned and cleared her throat. 'I must get on. Do you want me to come round with you?'

'If you would. Who's first?'

She accosted the notes trolley, straightened her shoulders and headed off towards the first patient.

'It's outrageous!'

'I think you'd look rather good in it, but if you don't like it how about this?'

Anna handed Tassy another gown, a ruched raspberry-coloured shot silk with a ballerina skirt. Tassy raised one brow. 'I don't think so,' she said drily.

'Not you?'

'Not me,' she said emphatically. 'Anna, I want something simple and classy and low-profile—you know, something with a front? And definitely no ballerina skirts.'

'Fine.'

Anna disappeared out of the fitting room and came back a moment later armed with another selection.

'How about this?'

'It's pink.'

'No pink?' Anna said, and Tassy shook her head. 'OK, no pink—well, how about this?'

'I look dead in yellow.'

Anna put her head on one side and growled at Tassy. 'It's a summer ball. You can't wear black.'

'So how about white—or cream? Just not frou-frou pink, for heaven's sake, or custard.'

'Frou-frou pink,' Anna muttered, stomping off. 'Custard.' A few moments later the curtain twitched back. 'Try this—it's absolutely my last offering. It looks like hell on the hanger and it would look horrendous on me, but I have a feeling that with your figure it'll be stunning. Put it on.'

Tassy took it almost reluctantly. It was a lovely

dress—cream silk, a very simple neckline with fine spaghetti straps and lots of crisscross straps across the low back, figure-hugging and straight to the ankles, with a kick-pleat to the knee on one side so she wouldn't have to walk like a geisha girl.

She didn't even dare look at the price. 'I can't wear a bra with it,' she said, eyeing it longingly.

'So don't.'

'Anna!' she said, scandalised. 'I have to wear a bra!'

'Why?'

'Because—well, because I do! There's just too much of me—'

'Oh, shut up and put it on. It might not fit, anyway.'

Anna snapped the curtain shut and stalked off. Tassy very dubiously took off her bra, slipped the dress over her head and wriggled into it. It had a side zip, and once it was done up and she'd tugged it straight she looked in the mirror.

'My God.'

'What?' The curtain whipped back and Anna stood there, her mouth open. 'Tassy, that's it. If you even try on anything else you're nuts.'

Tassy laughed awkwardly, eyeing herself from all angles. 'You're only saying that because you're sick of shopping with me.'

'Rubbish. If you can't see how good it is you deserve to be blind.'

Tassy ignored that and shook her head, peering over her shoulder. 'It's frightfully bare,' she said doubtfully.

'Bare nothing. It's a ball gown, not an overcoat. Anyway, it's got a little bolero-style jacket, if you think it's too bare. Here, stick this on.'

Tassy pulled on the little jacket and looked again. It

had a high mandarin neck, open down the front with the edges just meeting, and long, narrow sleeves that echoed the skirt. Anna was right—it was gorgeous, and she loved it to bits. She put it on her credit card, without even asking the price, and just hoped that when it came to the crunch she'd have the courage to wear it.

They hurried back to the hospital, and Tassy put the bag in her locker, pulled her tabard on over her uniform and went back out into the fray without giving the dress another thought.

Not that there was time to worry about a dress. A girl of ten was sent up from A and E, awaiting surgery for multiple fractures of her legs, and Tassy had to deal not only with the child but with her parents who were falling apart because the father had swung onto the drive and knocked the girl off her bike.

All three of them were crying. The mother was torn between berating the father and comforting the daughter, the father was alternating between defence of his actions and remorse at their consequences and the girl was just howling her eyes out because she was hurt and shocked.

Tassy deputised Anna to take the parents away to calm down and sign any necessary consent forms, had Ben paged to clerk her and did what she could in the meantime to make the child comfortable and prepare her for the surgery that was to follow.

She had been admitted under an orthopaedic firm but until a theatre was free she would have to stay on the ward. Her legs were supported in temporary splints and Tassy elevated them to prevent any further swelling and bleeding into the tissues. The moment Ben arrived he went over her with a fine-tooth comb to make sure she didn't have any sign of abdominal or head injuries.

They could hear the parents yelling even from across the ward, and Ben shot Tassy a meaningful glance. She nodded and, leaving the two of them, went into her office, closed the door and confronted the parents.

'Look, I realise you're both very shocked and upset,' she began, but the mother interrupted her.

'Shocked and upset? He nearly killed her! The times I've told him about swishing onto the drive like Damon Hill in a pitstop, but, oh, no, he can't slow down, he's always in too much of a hurry. Always a phone call to make or a deal to close or another unsuspecting punter to meet—'

'I hadn't noticed you complaining about the income! You might not like the way I earn it, but you're damn quick to spend it when it comes in! New car, new curtains, new clothes, another holiday, toys for the kids—'

'Would you both be quiet?' Tassy said furiously. 'Your daughter is lying out there with serious injuries, and you should be pulling together to support her instead of trying to apportion blame and airing old grievances!'

'What we need is a divorce!' the mother snapped.

'Fine,' Tassy replied, 'but perhaps you'd like to wait until your daughter's surgery is completed before you contact the solicitor? I really think you need to sit down, both of you, and just think about what's important here and what you're actually arguing about!'

She turned to Anna, who was standing there with her mouth slightly open. 'How are you getting on with the forms? We'll need them so she can go to Theatre the second they're ready for her.'

'Not wonderfully well,' Anna admitted. 'It's been a little difficult to hold their attention.'

Tassy turned back to the parents. 'We need as much

information as possible, please. The stuff from A and E was a little sketchy—perhaps you'd like to go over it all again with Staff Nurse Long here and make sure we've got everything we need. I'll get someone to bring you a cup of tea.'

She deputised one of the ward orderlies to make tea and then went back to Ben, who winked at her. 'Go, Tassy!' he murmured under his breath.

'Happy families,' she replied equally quietly, and moved up to the child's head.

'Sophie? Won't be long now, poppet. We'll soon have you comfy.'

'My bike's all bent,' she whispered. 'Mum'll kill me. It was new.'

Tassy patted her hand. 'I think you'll find your mum's much more worried about you than about your bike.'

Ben arched a disbelieving brow which Tassy ignored. She was much more concerned with keeping Sophie quiet and comfortable prior to surgery. She checked the drip, which was running in cross-matched blood to replace the large amount Sophie had lost into the tissues as a result of the fractures, and then checked the monitor on the wall behind.

Blood pressure normal, if a little low, temperature normal, respiration a little fast but nothing out of the ordinary—all she needed was to get down to Theatre and get fixed, and she'd be a lot better off.

One of the orthopaedic team came down and explained that she was having a pin in the left tibia or shin bone, and a plate and pin for the right tibia, which was shattered at the bottom and snapped halfway up as well. Because she was still growing the plate and pins would have to be removed when they had healed to prevent the bone growth from being affected, but that would be a much more simple operation.

He explained it to Sophie and her parents, who were now sitting quietly and apparently pulling together, and a short while later Sophie went off to Theatre.

She wasn't back by the time Tassy went off duty, but she was back with them and much brighter the following day, although in some pain. Tassy didn't feel Sophie could cope with the hurly-burly of the orthopaedic end where they had several fairly long-stay patients who were rather rowdy, and so she put her near Sam, who was out of his single room now and much happier with a little company.

He was allowed out of bed from time to time, and spent most of the day sitting beside Sophie and chatting to her when her parents weren't there.

They were considerably chastened after her telling-off, Tassy was pleased to note, although it was obvious they resented the fact that she'd had to tell them their job. At least, though, they were having their arguments elsewhere now.

Tassy was busy for the rest of that day and Saturday morning, which she was covering until lunchtime. Although a lot of the children in for operation were day cases or routine short-stay like tonsillectomy, glue-ear grommets and the like, there were others, of course, like Sophie and Sam and the orthopaedic crew, who were in for much longer, and they needed entertaining and nursing and watching.

Saturday mornings, though, were fun because there was no school and the hospital radio came down and chatted to the kids and interviewed them, to the delight of the other hospital patients. Tassy never minded working Saturdays, usually, except that today of all days she wanted time to go shopping and have her hair trimmed and buy some new tights and so on for the ball.

And, of course, there was the usual slather of reasons why she couldn't get away on time. She rushed into town, grabbed some glossy natural tights, some gold polish for her old strappy sandals and a new lipstick, and went home without a haircut because there just wasn't time.

Ben was lying on the drive with his head under the car when she arrived, and he wriggled out and grinned at her. 'Hi. Just took the dogs up to my parents and noticed a rattle—I think one of the exhaust brackets is dodgy. I was just trying to fix it.'

He glanced at his watch and then at her. 'It's nearly four. We ought to think about leaving at seven-thirty— do you want to have something light to eat now? Tea and toast or some such?'

She grinned at him. 'Are you offering to make it? I need to have a bath and wash my hair and try and do something with it unless I'm going to disgrace you.'

He laughed. 'I don't think there's any danger of that. Did you manage to find a dress?'

'Mmm.'

'What's it like?'

She smiled a little edgily. 'Nice, I think. I don't know. You'll see it soon enough.'

He muttered something that sounded like 'nothing like soon enough', and disappeared back under the car. 'Give me a shout when you get out of the bath—I'll make the tea,' he said from under the car, and she went in and bathed, laid out her underwear and checked that her dress had hung out all right, and then went next door in a pair of shorts and a T-shirt with her hair in a towel turban, to find that Ben had just made the tea.

She drank it fast, then disappeared back to her half of the house with a piece of toast in one hand and another mug of tea in the other to finish her preparations.

It took ages because she blow-dried her hair to curl under and applied her make-up with considerable care so she didn't get smudges under her eyes, and then it was time to put the dress on.

It was lined so she didn't need a slip, just the new glossy tights over a pair of the skimpiest, naughtiest silk knickers she'd ever worn in her life. She nearly bottled out but they were so fine and so minimal that she knew she couldn't possibly have a visible panty line, and so with a nervous laugh she pulled up the tights, smoothed down the dress and stood back.

'Oh, Lord, the top,' she muttered, just as the doorbell rang. She slipped on her sandals, hopped downstairs, tugging up the slingbacks, and opened the door to Ben as she was putting on the jacket.

'Wow.' He stepped in, shut the door and stared at her for a good ten seconds without another word until she began to squirm.

'Has it gone transparent or something?' she asked at last, uncomfortable with his scrutiny.

'Trans—' He cleared his throat and dragged his eyes up to hers. 'No, of course it hasn't gone transparent. It's fine. Beautiful. Fantastic. You look—'

'Ben, if you use another word like that I'll take it off. It's just a dress, for heaven's sake! Anyway, you're no slouch yourself. Now, can we go?'

He looked a little startled, but then a slow grin appeared on his lips and he nodded. 'Of course. Your chariot awaits.'

Damn. She hadn't meant to compliment him, but he did look wonderful in that dark dinner suit and finely pleated, blindingly white shirt. She'd better bring him back down to earth, though, she thought. Didn't want to give him ideas. 'Did you get the exhaust fixed?' she asked practically, to dampen him. It didn't work.

He grinned, pleased with himself. 'Yup. I'm nothing if not resourceful—I used a bit of coathanger wire. It'll do for the next few days, anyway.'

He limped over to the car, opened the door for her and helped her in. As he bent over to hand her the seat belt she caught a whiff of the citrus cologne he had used—good heavens, was it really only a week ago? The memory of that time with him made her heart trip, and when he turned his head and brushed her lips with his she thought it would stop altogether.

'OK?' he murmured.

'Yes,' Tassy replied, and then closed her eyes because her wretched voice had gone all squeaky and silly with anticipation. She was aching to dance with him, just to stand in his arms and sway to the music and forget, just for one evening, all the reasons why it was foolish to let her heart get involved.

By the time they arrived at the town hall people were streaming in, and he threaded his fingers through hers and held her close by his side. It might have been so he didn't lose her, or as a sort of masculine warning that she was his woman—whatever, it felt good to be so close to him and she was feeling charitable so she didn't want to question his motives.

They went inside with the glittering throng, and she

was suddenly glad she'd listened to Anna and bought the dress. They were sharing a table with Josh and Melissa Lancaster, Andrew and Jennifer Barrett and Joe and Thea Armitage, an 'obstetrics' couple Tassy knew slightly. Joe had apparently done Melissa's operation.

The women were all mothers, apart from Tassy, but it didn't stop them looking glamorous, and Melissa's dress particularly was very off-the-shoulder. Josh seemed to be thoroughly enjoying the view, but it didn't stop him admiring Tassy's dress and commenting that she looked lovely.

She felt the soft sweep of colour on her cheeks and opened her mouth to deny it, but Andrew interrupted her with a gentle reprimand. 'Tassy, it's time you learned to take a compliment, especially if you're going to look that beautiful,' he said with a kind smile, and she laughed self-consciously and turned to Josh and thanked him.

'Told you you looked good,' Ben murmured in her ear as he seated her.

'But you don't count,' she muttered back. 'You've got a vested interest in weakening my resistance.'

He chuckled, a low, throaty sound that did funny things to her insides. Then the background music faded, the emcee thanked everyone for coming, encouraged them to buy raffle tickets and without further ado introduced the band.

Ben turned to Tassy. 'I've waited since Thursday—I can't wait another minute. You and I are going to dance.'

Scooting back his chair, he got to his feet, held out his hand and led her to the dance floor. It was a lively number, but in deference to his knee, he said with a twinkle, they'd better make it a slow one.

So she found herself in his arms, where she'd been dreaming about being for a week, and with a little sigh she rested her cheek on his shoulder, allowed him to ease her closer so their bodies moved as one and let her fantasies run riot.

They did—big-time. She remembered the touch of his hand, the slow caress of his eyes, the feel of his skin, the soft, supple glide of it over the firm-toned muscles underneath. She remembered the slightly coarse texture of the hair that scattered his body in places, and imagined the feel of that hair chafing against her own much softer skin as their legs tangled—

A tiny moan rose in her throat, and he eased her even closer so that she could feel that he, too, was remembering and suffering.

'This is going to be one hell of a long night,' he murmured in her ear, and she laughed, a breathless, slightly strangled little sound full of desperation.

He squeezed her gently, then eased her away a fraction. 'I don't want to disgrace myself,' he said with a rueful smile, and she had to make do with almost touching him for the rest of the dance.

And the one after, and the one after that, until in the end neither of them could stand the frustration any longer and they went and sat down, chatted to the others and ate their buffet supper.

It grew hotter in the big room, and Tassy was forced to slip off the little jacket. Ben's eyes tracked over her bare shoulders, then locked with hers, their message clear. She looked away but felt his fingertips trailing over the bare skin of her back where his arm was draped along the back of her chair. She leant forward, out of his reach, and he laughed softly.

'Fraidy-cat,' he murmured in a sing-song voice.

She gave him a quelling look—or tried to. It didn't really work. He just smiled knowingly, dropped his hand down the back of the chair and rested it possessively on her hip.

Josh, watching the by-play from the other side of the table, stood up and grinned at Tassy, holding out his hand to her. 'We have to go soon because Melissa's tired, but before we do I simply have to dance with you in that wonderful dress.'

Tassy stood up and let him draw her onto the dance floor, conscious of Ben's frown and Melissa's indulgent smile. Oh, yes, she knows she's well loved and cherished, Tassy thought, and felt a pang of something akin to envy. God knows they deserved their happiness, but it was so rare and precious. She wondered if they knew just how lucky they were to have found each other.

Josh took her in his arms, holding her close but not too close, maintaining a discreet and comfortable distance between them. Funny, he was absolutely gorgeous—all of the nurses and mothers fell for him instantly—and yet being held like this by him did nothing for her at all. He was a colleague, nothing more, and she was genuinely fond of him.

And yet Ben...

'You sure you're OK?'

She smiled up at him, amused and yet touched at his concern. 'I'm fine, Josh.'

'OK. I'm just making sure. If you want a lift home or anything...'

She looked up at him in astonishment. 'Why would I

want a lift home? Josh, I don't know what's happening between us, but I know he won't hurt me. I'm more likely to hurt myself by falling for a dream.'

'What?' Josh bent closer, unable to hear over the music, and she shook her head.

'I'm fine, Josh. Don't be a worry-wart.'

The song came to an end, and he slipped his arm round her shoulders, gave her a quick squeeze and led her back to the table.

'Back in a tick,' he said to Melissa, then jerked his head at Ben and left them.

Ben, raising an eyebrow at Tassy in enquiry, followed him.

'I think Josh is playing the heavy uncle,' Tassy said uncomfortably to Melissa. The others were on the dance floor and they were alone, and Melissa smiled sympathetically at her.

'Sorry. He worries about you. He'll only warn him not to break your heart.'

Tassy gave a choked laugh. 'That's what I'm afraid of! Poor Ben.'

'I'm sure poor Ben can cope with it,' Melissa said drily. 'He looks pretty tough to me.'

They reappeared, neither of them sporting obvious injuries, and Josh and Melissa left.

'What was that all about?' Tassy asked him.

Ben looked uncomfortable. 'He threatened to kill me if I got you pregnant.'

Tassy's heart thumped. Hopefully it wasn't already too late. She tried to reassure Ben about Josh's murderous intent. 'He got Melissa pregnant,' she told him.

'They *are* married.'

'They weren't.'

Ben smiled slowly. 'Really? How interesting. You'd never know it to hear him talk about family values and protecting the virtue of the innocent.'

Tassy gave a wry laugh. 'Perhaps he should have spoken to you a week ago.'

'He speaks to me every other day. He's very protective. I think he imagines you need a champion.'

'Or a bodyguard. He was watching us dance, and he was glaring at you when you were groping me.'

'I was hardly groping you, darling.'

Darling? Her heart thumped. It sounded so wonderful, until she remembered the circles he'd mixed in. Artistic people called each other darling all the time—usually with an aitch in the middle. It meant nothing. Nothing at all.

Ben, oblivious to the tumult inside her, swirled his drink in his glass and looked across at her. 'Do you think he fancies you himself?'

'No,' she said instantly. 'No, I know he doesn't. He adores Melissa. He's just one of those people who has to look after everyone. He does it all the time. He's a wonderful father—a natural.'

Ben was quiet for a moment, then looked up and spoke, his voice a little gruff. 'I want to dance with you again, but I'm not sure I dare.'

'Because of Josh?' she said, astonished.

He laughed briefly. 'No, because of me—because of you. Because of what happens to us when we get that close, especially now I've seen what that dress is really like.' He reached out and covered her hand with his. 'Tassy, come home with me,' he murmured.

The invitation in his eyes was unmistakable—and irresistible.

She picked up her jacket and the little evening purse
with her lipstick in, and smiled. 'Come on, then,' she
said. 'What are you waiting for?'

CHAPTER NINE

IT WAS everything Tassy had remembered, and more. She was scared to death, dreading that she was making a mistake, that it wouldn't be as she'd remembered it and that it would all go wrong, or that at the last minute Ben would decide he didn't find her attractive and didn't want her after all.

She should have saved her energy. She needed it. Ben was demanding, despite the constraints of his injured knee, and he drove her to heights she hadn't known existed.

Afterwards she felt shy, a little stunned by her uninhibited response, but he seemed to understand. His touch gentle, he drew her close against his side and kissed her lingeringly. 'I've missed you this week,' he murmured. 'Funny how you can get addicted to someone in just one night.'

She didn't find it funny, she found it faintly terrifying. It had been hard to keep a distance before tonight. Now it would be well nigh impossible, and she was sure he would try and make it so.

She wasn't wrong. He kissed her again, one leg flung possessively across hers, a hand curled over her hipbone, anchoring her at his side.

'Tassy, move in with me,' he said quietly.

She'd known it was coming, and she was ready for it, but it hurt her nevertheless to say no because a little bit of her that wanted to believe in happy-ever-after was clamouring to say yes.

'Ben, I can't,' she explained, ignoring that little noisy bit. 'I need my space. It's too soon. I need my independence—I can't sacrifice everything. I know just what'll happen—we'd open up the house, muddle all our things up and then something will go wrong and I'll have to move out, and it won't be possible to go back to my part of the house because it won't be separate any more, and—'

'Tassy?'

She stopped protesting and turned her head slightly. His eyes, brilliant green and searching, were inches from hers. 'Why will things go wrong?'

She closed her eyes. She couldn't bear to rehash all the hurt Derek had inflicted, especially not now, lying here in Ben's arms slaked from their lovemaking. 'Ben, please. I don't want to move in—not yet, at least.'

'And what about this?' he asked, running his hand softly up over the curve of her ribs to settle possessively around her breast. 'Will I still be allowed to make love to you, or was tonight just an aberration?'

Her nipple peaked against the teasing of his thumb, and he bent his head and drew it deep into his mouth, suckling hard but not quite hard enough to hurt her. She cried out, and he shifted his attention to the soft skin of her throat, over the racing pulse that gave him his answer.

'Stay the night,' he murmured against her skin, ruthlessly pressing his advantage, and she gave in, as he must have known she would.

Rat that he was, he hadn't left her any choice…

* * *

The week was hellish. It started with problems with Sam, who was beginning to find his grossly restricted activity irksome. Andrew Barrett decided he was well enough to start lessons with the teacher, and so she came to him and Sophie on Monday afternoon.

By then, of course, Sam was tired and irritable and needed his sleep so it wasn't an altogether successful session, but it was a start. As his heart was sounding and looking good, and his pain and involuntary movements had subsided as well, they also decided to step up his physiotherapy in the hope that that would build him up and give him more stamina.

'But I already have physio,' Sam said, when Tassy tried to explain what they were going on to do next with him.

Tassy shook her head. 'This is different. You know she's been giving you exercises to keep your joints moving when they haven't been sore? Well, now you're a bit better Dr Lazaar thinks you should be doing a bit more to make your heart work harder and build up your muscles again.'

Sam's little face creased with concern. 'But I thought I couldn't do anything much because it would hurt my heart?' he said worriedly.

Tassy smiled and squeezed his hand reassuringly. 'Don't worry, you won't be doing very much, and it's quite safe now—you're getting better.'

He still looked doubtful, and Sue, the physio, reported to Tassy that he was very reluctant to do the exercises.

'I think maybe we've made too big a thing about resting so that he's now scared to do anything else.'

Tassy sighed. 'I'll get Ben to talk to him again. How's Sophie getting on?'

The physio was coming to Sophie as well, to keep her upper body moving and encourage movement of her multi-coloured toes. 'OK, fine,' Sue said, pulling a face. 'Obviously she's pretty sore and I have to take it very steadily, but she's quite cooperative. Her mother was there—is she a bit scared of her?'

Tassy thought back to the fight she and her husband had had the day of Sophie's accident, and rolled her eyes. 'She's not a very gentle or giving woman, I don't think. I imagine she makes quite a fuss about keeping things tidy and doing things right, and I think the children get into trouble if they break things.'

Sue laughed. 'But not their legs, surely?'

'No,' Tassy said drily, 'it was the husband that got in trouble for that, but Sophie was worried about the bike being damaged and said her mother would kill her.'

Sue shook her head. 'Parents,' she groaned. 'Sometimes I think the kids would be better off without them.'

Tassy thought of the quiet, gentle woman who loved Sam to distraction. 'Not always,' she said. 'Anyway, what are you going to do about Sam?'

'Just persevere gently. I thought it would be easy to do a few minutes with him without him getting too tired or stressed as I'm just there with Sophie and he knows me, but we'll have to see. Get Ben to have another chat with him, if you could.'

She assured Sue she would, but there wasn't another opportunity until that evening when she was at home. She waited till Ben was out in the garden, sprawled in the hammock with his bandaged knee stretched out in front of him, and hopped over the little fence.

'Hi,' he said with a smile, and went to sit up. Tassy pushed him down with a firm hand on his bare shoulder.

'Don't move. I don't want you falling out of there again and blaming me. It's about Sam.'

'Oh. How disappointing. I thought you were coming to tell me you found my body irresistible and wanted to join me in here.'

She snorted. 'In your dreams.' She outlined Sue's problem, trying very hard to keep her eyes off his near-naked body and her mind on the job.

'I'll talk to him,' Ben promised, and reached out for her hand. 'Come and join me.'

She shook her head but he gave her hand a little tug and she fell into the hammock, sprawling on top of him with a complete absence of dignity.

'Ben,' she protested, struggling to sit up, but he pulled her down to his mouth and kissed her. With a little sigh she relaxed against him, and within seconds he had engineered a complete disintegration of her resolve. It really was ridiculous, she thought later as she lay there with him under the willow in the cool of the night, how little self-control she had when she was around him. No wonder she'd chucked herself at him with such indecent haste. At least this time, though, they'd both remembered the sixty million opportunities for conception—if it wasn't already too late.

By Wednesday there was still no sign of her period, and Tassy began to wonder if she had made a mistake with her dates. After all, with no reason to monitor her cycle it was something that tended to happen without any fuss, and so it was easy to misremember. She knew it was a weekend, but which one?

She put the worry to the back of her mind, carried on with her work and allowed herself to enjoy Ben's attentions in the evenings.

Not every evening, though. Tempting though it was, she didn't allow herself to be talked into spending all her free time with him. He was often busy, anyway, revising for exams or doing coursework set as part of his training as a special registrar, and so he didn't push her if she said no.

It was just as well because her resolve was a pretty feeble thing these days, and no wonder. He was the most amazing lover. With her vast absence of knowledge and experience, Tassy knew it was hard to tell, but she was pretty sure that most men weren't as considerate and generous—or as downright sexy.

She didn't regret not moving in, though. In many ways it was nice to sit in her own little room with the doors open and listen to the summer evenings, without having to make conversation or look alluring.

Not that she did. Often they sat in companionable silence, but she wondered if he would get bored with her if she didn't scintillate a bit every now and then so it was lovely to be able to doze or watch television or just plain do nothing.

By the end of the weekend there was still no sign of her period, and she went back to work on Monday morning feeling rather subdued and worried. Her system, usually so regular and reliable, had failed. She put the worry on the back burner yet again, and somehow got through the next few days.

Sophie and Sam were getting on well, and as both of them needed quite a bit of rest Tassy arranged the other little patients to give them a small area to themselves where they could be quiet in the afternoons.

Sam was accepting his physio now after talking to Ben, and was quite happy to be doing a bit more to pass the time. Sophie, though, was getting bored as she adjusted to the enforced inactivity, and the occupational therapist came and talked to her to see if she could find something that Sophie could do. They went through her kits of soft toys and Sophie chose a little white kitten with startlingly blue eyes and a blue collar and bell.

'It'll take me ages,' Sophie said to Tassy on Friday afternoon, after Tassy had helped her unpick a wrongly joined seam.

'You'll get there,' she said with a smile. 'Look—it's beginning to come together already. Keep going.'

Ben paused beside her, admired Sophie's handiwork and then walked with Tassy back to her office.

'Doing anything tonight?' he asked her once the door was closed.

Buying a pregnancy test kit, but she wasn't telling him that.

'Why?' she asked casually, busying herself with something so she didn't have to meet his eyes when her own were full of evasion.

He shrugged. 'Wondered if you fancied a pub meal by a river somewhere. It's so hot—what do you think?'

She shook her head. 'No, thanks, I'm really quite tired.' And I have other, more monumental things to do.

'Pasta and salad in the garden at home?'

She smiled wryly at his persistence but still shook her head. 'No, Ben, sorry. I just need a quiet night in on my own.'

'You had one of them last night.'

'Am I rationed?' she asked, a touch irritated and with worry shortening her fuse even further.

He stepped back a pace and threw up his hands.

'Sorry. Didn't mean to crowd you. Perhaps some time over the weekend.'

Perhaps, she thought. She had a feeling she'd have some difficult decisions to make very shortly, and whether or not to involve him in them was the first.

She picked up the test from the chemist, went home and opened it in the privacy of her bathroom. It seemed enormously straightforward. Basically all she had to do was pee on the little stick, wait for a few minutes and see if a blue line appeared a certain distance up it.

Just like that, her life would be rearranged.

She sat for ages staring at this little stick and wondering if she wanted to know, if she was being silly and had got her dates totally wrong, but she knew she wasn't that bad at maths. She was at least one week overdue, if not two, and there was no getting away from it. The test would just stop her denying it any longer.

And that, of course, was the trouble.

She put the kit down, went and made a drink, changed out of her uniform into a cool, loose T-shirt dress and went back to the bathroom. It was no good, she had to know.

She checked the instructions again unnecessarily, followed them to the letter and waited.

'Oh, hell,' she muttered, and sat down on the edge of the bath with a little plonk.

Positive.

She was going to have a baby.

Ben's baby.

A little spurt of joy penetrated the shock and confusion, and put the whole thing into perspective.

A baby wasn't a disaster. It was a miracle, and she was suddenly enormously relieved that the test hadn't been negative. All she had to do now was decide if she'd involve Ben.

She wished she had a mother she could talk to, instead of the coldly distant and disappointed relative God had seen fit to provide her with. She really needed someone's love and support just now.

Ben's would be nice.

She shut her eyes and gave a little whimper of despair and confusion. She felt scared, she felt tired and she felt—

Sick.

It must be psychological, she thought as she lifted her head out of the toilet bowl and crawled back onto the side of the bath. Just because you know, you think you ought to be sick. She washed her face, stared once again at the little stick with its telltale blue line and threw the kit in the kitchen bin.

No. Ben might find it there if he came in. She took the bin liner out of the little bin and put it outside in her big dustbin, then made herself a simple supper. Tea, toast and honey and a yoghurt.

It stayed down. In fact, she felt better for having eaten, and sat staring at the television for ages without seeing it before she went to bed, thinking about the baby and the changes that were coming in her life.

She slept like a log, lying in long past her usual time to get up even at the weekends, able to sleep again now she had her answer. It was Ben's knock at her door that woke her.

'Tassy?' he called.

She stumbled out of bed, pushed back her hair and hurried downstairs to open the door. 'Sorry, I overslept,' she told him drowsily. 'Come in.'

His eyes tracked over her nightshirt and bare legs, and back to her face. Idiot, she thought, I must look like hell.

'My parents are here,' he told her. 'They'd like to meet you, and they wanted to see the cottage.'

She looked around it in horror and swallowed. 'Give me an hour, can you?'

'Sure. Join us for coffee when you're ready.'

It was the word 'coffee' that did it. She pasted a quick smile on her face, shut the door and bolted to the loo just in time.

Funnily enough, she thought a while later as she tidied up the house and ran the vacuum cleaner over it, once she'd been sick she was fine. She'd had breakfast and something to drink, but not coffee, and she was OK now.

Just as well, because the place needed a major sort-out before she'd let Ben's mother within a hundred miles of it!

Finally satisfied with its appearance, she went out of the French doors, hopped over the fence and joined them by the willow.

'Oh, you've got the dogs!' she exclaimed, as Ben leapt up at her and nearly knocked her over. 'Ben, get down!'

He subsided to the floor with a wiggle, and she laughed and patted him, before turning her attention to Ben's parents.

Oh, yes. It was easy to see where he came from. He was the spitting image of his father, with the exception of his mother's hair colour and those astonishing green eyes—eyes that were assessing her with open curiosity.

Ben introduced them as David and Joan, and his mother smiled welcomingly and offered her a coffee.

'Actually, it feels a bit hot for coffee—do you mind

if I have mineral water?' she said, swallowing hard and forcing a smile. Even the thought—

'There's some in the fridge,' Ben told her so she went and poured herself a glass and took it back out. Belatedly it occurred to her to wonder exactly what Ben had told his parents about her, but she decided to take her cue from him and play it by ear. Maybe, with any luck, he had only told them that she was his tenant and that they worked together.

After they'd drunk their coffee and she'd sipped her mineral water and tried to look inconspicuous and like a tenant, Ben turned to his parents. 'Fancy a guided tour of the estate, then?' he said with a grin.

'Lovely,' his mother said instantly. His father concurred, and then Ben looked at Tassy.

'Is it all right if I show them round your part?'

'Of course,' she replied, hoping it was clean and tidy enough to pass those eagle eyes.

She needn't have worried. They didn't actually get that far because Bill and Ben went bounding round the corner of the house, knocked over her dustbin and there on the ground in front of their feet was the box from the pregnancy test.

She bent down quickly to shove it and everything else back into the bin, but one of the dogs was too quick for her and grabbed the box and legged it down the garden.

Good, she thought, maybe he'll eat it and destroy the evidence, and she pushed everything else back into the bin, before straightening up. 'Come on in,' she invited breezily, opening the door and hoping they would leave the dog in peace to finish his stolen prize. The dog, however, had other ideas. Bored with that game, he bounded into the house, went straight up to Ben's father and sat down in front of him, dropping the box at his feet.

Tassy's heart dropped to the floor with it. Being a retriever, of course, he'd been gentle with it, and the box was quite unmarked and thus perfectly recognisable.

Dr Lazaar bent down, picked it up and handed it to Tassy without a word, but their eyes locked and she knew he'd realised what it was.

So had Ben and his mother, and in the silence that followed a dropped pin would have been deafening.

'Tassy?' Ben said softly after an age.

She drew in a steadying breath, lifted her head and met the blaze of hope and suspense in his eyes.

'Yes,' she said simply.

He sat down with a plonk on the arm of the sofa. 'My God.' He looked down at his hands, then back at her, and there was a suspicious gleam of moisture in his eyes. 'A baby.' He laughed, a short, stunned laugh that cracked at the end, and then he swept her up into his arms and spun her round, kissing her soundly before setting her back on her feet. 'We're going to have a baby,' he said in wonderment, and hugged her again, before turning to his parents.

'You're going to be grandparents again, guys.'

David and Joan Lazaar looked from Ben to Tassy to each other, and then Mrs Lazaar burst into tears. 'Oh, Ben,' she wept, pressing a hand to her mouth. 'I thought I was going to die without seeing you married and settled—I can't believe it. It's wonderful.'

'I'm not that old,' he laughed, and then the laughter drained from his face, taking the colour with it. 'My God, you mean it! Mum, explain. What are you talking about?'

She pulled herself together and wiped her eyes. 'I wasn't going to tell you—'

'Tell me what?' Ben said in a curiously flat voice.

'She found another lump,' his father told him gently. 'She's having a biopsy done in two weeks.'

Ben sat down on the arm again as if someone had cut his strings, and Tassy felt the chill of shock run through him as if it were her own. His face white, he stared at his mother in disbelief. 'I thought you were clear?' he said gruffly.

'I was. It may be nothing, but when you've faced breast cancer you never really believe you've beaten it. Oh, dear, I wasn't going to tell you, darling. I didn't want to worry you, but it just came out.' She smiled and patted his shoulder. 'It's probably nothing.'

'They don't biopsy nothings,' Ben said tightly, hanging onto Tassy's hand like a lifeline. She could feel the fear in him, the dread that his mother, whom he obviously loved, would be snatched from him, and she squeezed his hand back in silent support. 'What did the consultant say?'

'That it might well be nothing. Ben, I've had innocent cysts before now. I'm just overreacting. Ignore me. Let's talk about the baby.'

'I suppose it's not politically correct to discuss marriage at this point,' his father said wryly, picking up his wife's cue.

'Oh, David, of course it is,' Joan said, her eyes misting. 'Anyone can see they're head over heels. The only thing is when. Soon, of course, for obvious reasons, except I'm having this biopsy, but, still, it's on a Monday—'

'Mother, I think you're getting ahead of yourself,' Ben

interrupted gently. 'It might be an idea to allow me time to propose to Tassy before you choose the colour of your dress. You are rather assuming that we're going to get married.'

She stared at him, looking stunned. 'But of course you're going to get married! Why ever would you not?'

'Maybe she doesn't love me,' Ben said quietly, still hanging onto Tassy's hand like grim death.

Tassy opened her mouth to protest that of course she loved him, thought better of it and closed it again.

Mrs Lazaar opened and shut hers as well, and tried again. 'Of course she loves you. She couldn't fail to love you!'

'Carla did.'

She shook her head. 'Darling, Carla only loved herself. I told you that at the beginning, but you're a slow learner. Tassy's lovely and she adores you. Don't you, Tassy?'

Tassy couldn't speak. She looked at Ben for help, and he shut his eyes and sighed, then looked his mother squarely in the eye. 'Mother, stop it,' he pleaded. 'She might want to say no. Don't make it difficult for her.'

That clinched it for Tassy. If he'd pushed, if he'd used his mother's enthusiasm or illness to help sweep her along, she would have panicked. The fact that he was prepared to fight her corner for her made all the difference. She wasn't ready yet to tell him that she loved him, but he would be a wonderful father and it was beyond her to deny a possibly dying woman the happiness she could so easily give her.

'Of course I'll marry you,' she said to Ben, and all hell broke loose...

*   *   *

'You're a fool,' she told herself later. 'A sentimental, soft-hearted fool. How can you marry him? He only thinks he loves you—you said yourself you'd never get married again, and here you are, throwing yourself into it after only five weeks! How can you possibly know him well enough after five weeks? You didn't know Derek well enough after five months!'

But Ben wasn't Derek. He was nothing like him, and that was the only thing that gave her hope in the midst of all the chaos that ensued.

He told everyone at work, of course—that is to say, he told Anna, and Anna spread it like wildfire round the department. He didn't mention the baby, but it took Josh one searching look to work it out.

'Come for lunch,' he told her, and whisked her off without time to protest. They left the hospital, drove to a garage and bought sandwiches and mineral water, and found a quiet spot on the edge of town overlooking heathland.

'So, tell me all about it,' he said softly.

'There's not a lot to tell.'

'Except that you're marrying him because you're pregnant.'

She let her breath out in a gust. 'Yes—six weeks or so.'

'That was pretty swift work for someone like you who doesn't even go to the pub with friends.'

She blushed, ashamed of herself, and he covered her hands. 'That wasn't a criticism,' he said gently. 'When it comes to hasty courtships we've got the rest of the world licked. Melissa got pregnant the weekend we met.'

'At least we waited a fortnight,' she said with a shaky laugh.

'Positively staid,' Josh teased, and then his smile faded and he leant back against his door, searching her face with his perceptive eyes. 'So, what's the problem, Tassy, because there is one. I can tell it isn't all sunshine and roses.'

She shrugged. 'I keep wondering if it's a good enough reason to get married.'

'It was good enough for me. Of course it helped that I loved Melissa and had done since I first met her. How do you feel about Ben?'

'I love him,' she confessed, able to tell him what she wasn't able to tell Ben himself.

'And does he love you?'

'He says so.'

Josh frowned at her thoughtfully. 'Don't you believe him?'

She shrugged. 'I don't know. I don't know whether to believe him or not. He wants this dream so badly, Josh, I don't know if he's just kidding himself. He's had women in the past who didn't want to know when it came to the crunch. I think he's just latched onto me because he feels I'm a carer, and that I might be able to dream his dream with him.'

'And could you?'

She laughed, her eyes filling with tears. 'Oh, yes, Josh, so easily. I just can't believe it's real, though, and I'm so scared that it isn't.'

'I'm sure you'll grow to love each other more, even if you think you don't yet. So long as you both pull in the same direction, have the same dream—that's what counts.'

She swallowed the sudden lump in her throat. 'I hope you're right, Josh, or it's going to be a lot of heartache all round.' She turned to him and took his hand. 'Josh, you know I haven't got a father any more—would you give me away?'

'Me?' He coloured slightly and his eyes seemed even brighter. 'Tassy, I'd be honoured,' he said gruffly. 'Really honoured. And if you decide you don't want to go through with it just let me know and I'll help you sort it all out and find somewhere to live—OK? Just remember who your friends are.'

Her eyes filled, and this time she couldn't keep the tears in. They splashed down her cheeks and she reached over and hugged him. 'Thanks, Josh,' she whispered. 'I'll remember.'

CHAPTER TEN

'OH, TASSY, tell me, are the dogs all right?'

Tassy sat down beside Mrs Gates and patted her hand reassuringly. 'They're fine. They came and saw us at the weekend and they were getting on really well.'

'And are they being good?'

'As far as I know.' She didn't mention the part Ben had played in revealing her pregnancy, but she didn't feel like discussing it with Mrs Gates, anyway. She hardly knew her well enough to discuss something so intimate so she shifted the subject back to the woman herself.

'So, tell me, how are you getting on? How are the hips?'

'Oh, so much better. You'd be amazed. The first day I wondered what on earth I'd done, but after that it was wonderful. Marvellous.' She laughed. 'Mind you, I can't do a thing for myself, and after eighty-three years of being independent—and a widow for forty-seven of them—that takes a bit of getting used to. Still, it'll be better before long, I'm sure.'

'I would enjoy it while the going's good,' Tassy advised with a laugh. 'I'd love to be waited on for a while.'

'Get that nice young man of yours to wait on you—he tells me you're very independent and stubborn but he loves you, anyway. You ought to marry him—he's a good-looking young fellow and he's got good prospects. You could do a lot worse.'

Tassy gave a rather weak smile. 'Actually, we are going to get married. He asked me at the weekend.' In front of his parents, the dogs and a pregnancy test kit.

'Oh, my dear, how wonderful. Well, I'm sure you'll be very happy. I'm sure I would if someone that handsome wanted to marry me!' She chuckled, and Tassy pasted on a smile and tried not to think about the real reason they were getting married. She suddenly wished with all her heart that he was marrying her just because he wanted to, without the complication of her pregnancy—and then a hideous, sickly thought occurred to her.

What if he had been backing off in front of his parents not because he didn't want to push her into it but because he himself didn't want to be pushed? What if he'd only been telling her he loved her to keep her where he wanted her—in bed? What if it was just a line he used? She only had his word for it that there'd been only two other women in his life. Was that a line, too?

Suddenly swamped with dread and nausea, she excused herself hastily from Mrs Gates and almost ran off the orthopaedic ward and into the loo. A few moments in there cured the nausea, but it did nothing for the dread.

She tried to think it through rationally. What if it wasn't a line, but he was only marrying her to make his dying mother happy?

If she was dying. What if they found out from the biopsy that she was all right? Would they know in time to stop the wedding? Or did he just want to marry her for the baby so he could have his dream?

There were so many ifs, so many buts, so many maybes.

She got up off her knees, washed her face and went back to the ward. She'd missed lunch, but she couldn't eat—

'You look like hell.'

'Thank you. I feel much better now.'

Ben drew her into the treatment room and looked down into her face with a worried frown. 'Are you feeling sick?'

'Not any more.'

'You need to eat.'

'Don't tell me—you're an expert on morning sickness.'

'No, my mother is. She told me you need to suck ice and eat rich tea biscuits and slices of chilled apple and peeled grapes because they've got lots of sugar to get your blood sugar up. And you need rest, and no worries, and time with your feet up.'

She rolled her eyes. 'Fine. Ben, that's basically incompatible with life and, anyway, who's going to peel me grapes?'

'You'd be surprised.'

She made a rude noise. 'Look, I have work to do. If you're going to hold me up it'll just add to my stress levels.'

'OK. First of all, though, I want you to help me. We've got a kid who's just on his way up from A and E with massive injuries to the hand and arm. He was lift-surfing—riding on top of the lift inside the shaft—when he caught his hand on a moving flywheel and virtually tore it off. He's going to be going to Theatre shortly, but he's coming here to stabilise while he waits. We need to take bloods for cross-matching and keep his mother calm—she's absolutely beside herself.'

Tassy felt sick again. 'How old?' she asked, dredging up her professionalism.

'Ten.'

'We seem to get a lot of ten-year-olds with no sense,' she muttered. 'I wonder what it is about the magic age of ten that gives kids a death wish?'

It was a rhetorical question, but it was just as well because there wasn't time to answer. They heard the weeping, distraught mother before the squeak of the trolley wheels, and then the A and E nurse was handing over the notes and the child and making her escape.

Tassy took one look at the blood-stained stump on the end of the boy's left arm and took the mother into the office, clutching the notes like a lifeline.

'Right, Mrs Zerilli, we need to admit Laurence. I want as much information as you can give me.'

'I don't know why he do this stupid thing!' she wailed. 'Oh, Lord, help me, my boy's gonna die—'

'Mrs Zerilli, he's not going to die, but I do need some information.' She opened the A and E notes and saw a scribbled postscript.

'Unable to extract any information from distraught Italian mother.'

Tassy shook her head. 'Mrs Zerilli, where do you live?'

'I knew I shouldn't let him out with that boy—he's trouble for sure, I knew that. Oh, Laurence, don' die, son!' she wailed, and collapsed in a fresh wave of sobbing.

Tassy left her there for a moment and went out to find Ben. 'I can't do a thing with her—can you prescribe something to calm her down? She's absolutely beside herself.'

'Give her ten milligrams of diazepam and a cup of tea, and maybe you'll have some joy in about half an hour. Did they give her anything in A and E?'

'Dunno—I'll check. Thanks.'

She went back into her office, where Anna was trying to persuade Mrs Zerilli to drink some tea, and phoned A and E. They hadn't given her anything, so Tassy unlocked the drugs cupboard. 'Ten milligrams of diazepam, Ben says. Here you are, Mrs Zerilli, take this. It'll make you feel better soon.'

She put the pill in the woman's mouth, and Anna held the teacup while she slurped the liquid distractedly. She was still crying, and Tassy wondered how on earth they would get her calm enough to talk to before the boy had to go to Theatre.

'Mrs Zerilli, can you help us? Laurence has to go to the operating theatre in a minute, and we need you to sign a form to say that they can give him an operation.'

'They gonna take his arm off, I know they are!' she wailed, and collapsed again.

'No, Mrs Zerilli, they're going to stop the bleeding and clean it up and repair it as much as they can, but they can't just leave him. Now, please sign this form so that they can—'

'I don't want no surgeon cuttin' my boy up!' she protested. 'They cut his hand off for sure—'

'Mrs Zerilli, they will only do whatever is necessary to save his life and make his arm as useful as possible. They won't cut off anything that isn't too badly damaged to repair—'

'His father gonna kill him—'

'Mrs Zerilli, if you don't sign this form so he can go

to Theatre, you're going to kill him because he'll die from loss of blood!' Tassy said emphatically.

Behind the woman Ben had come to a halt and raised his eyebrows in amazement.

'Please, Mrs Zerilli, sign it,' she begged, pushing the form under the woman's nose.

'You promise me they won't do nothin' they don't have to?'

'I promise.'

'They can't sew his hand back?'

Tassy raised a brow at Ben but he shook his head emphatically. 'No, I'm sorry, but they'll do everything they can. Now, please, sign the form and then you can go and say goodbye to him before he goes up to Theatre.'

At last the form was signed, the boy was despatched, Mrs Zerilli had fallen asleep in a chair in the day room and Tassy sagged back against a chair in the treatment room and closed her eyes.

'Still feeling rough?'

'Would you believe rougher?' she said, without opening her eyes. 'I thought pregnancy was supposed to be a sign of health.'

Ben chuckled. 'That's what they always say.'

She opened her eyes a crack and dragged herself to her feet. 'I feel shattered, Ben. I thought that woman was going to pass out with hysterics before she signed the form.'

'It was a pretty devastating thing to have to deal with. You imagine your precious son, apple of your eye, rips his hand off—'

'OK, Ben, thanks, I get the picture.'

He peered at her. 'Are you a tad queasy about this? Have you gone squeamish?'

'Apparently,' she growled, heading towards her office. 'Now I'm going to go and do a nice, sensible, quiet drugs round with Anna, and then I think I might just slide off early and put my feet up.'

'Have you seen one of the obstetricians yet?'

She stopped walking and turned to face him. 'Ben, I'm only just pregnant. I haven't even seen a GP yet.'

He grinned and threw up his hands. 'OK. Sorry. When you do go may I come with you?'

She stared at him for a moment, then lifted her shoulders in a little shrug. 'Yes, I suppose so. You are the father.'

'Do you mind?'

'That you're the father, or that you want to come?'

He gave a little laugh. 'Either. Both.'

She looked down at her hands. 'I don't know. No, I don't think so. Ben, I don't feel up to this. I have to get on.'

Tassy did only what she absolutely had to do, but she still only got away half an hour early. She went home, poured herself a nice tall glass of mineral water, found a packet of rich tea biscuits and settled down in front of the television.

Two hours later she woke up with a stiff neck, a cold wet patch where she'd spilt the drink on her chest and a soggy packet of biscuits.

Ben was standing at her French doors, a tray in his hands, and she struggled to her feet, offloading the soggy biscuits and empty glass on the way, and let him in.

'What happened to you?' he asked.

'I fell asleep—what are you, my fairy godmother? What's under the cloth?'

'Goodies. I'm assuaging my guilt because it's my baby that's making you feel rotten.'

Tassy hoped she was going to be able to eat enough to make the effort worthwhile, but when she lifted the cloth she was stunned. There was a bowl of halved, peeled grapes, another of apple slivers in ice and lemon, some crackers and, of all things, a little pot of Gentlemen's Relish.

'Anchovies are very salty—my mother used to love Gentlemen's Relish when she was pregnant, she told me.'

Tassy, highly suspicious, tried a little streak of it on a cracker and surprised herself by liking it. She had another cracker, then another, followed by some of the grapes, and after a last slice of apple she keeled over on the sofa and sighed. 'That was wonderful—thanks.'

He put the tray down and perched on the edge of a chair. 'Why don't you go to bed?' he suggested.

'I can't be bothered to move,' she admitted. 'Did Laurence Zerilli come back from Theatre?'

'Yes. They couldn't save any of his hand, but they sorted out his arm to leave him a useful stump for a prosthesis. The bad news is he's left-handed, but he's only young so he can soon learn to use the other one.'

'What a stupid thing to do.'

'Kids can be stupid. I did some crazy things when I was a child.'

'Not like that, though.'

He smiled wryly. 'Perhaps not quite as daft, but pretty hair-raising. I climbed a pylon once and nearly got electrocuted, and I used to play chicken on the railway line.'

Tassy closed her eyes. 'I don't suppose there's any danger this baby will just take after me? I never did anything crazy in my childhood—in fact, until I met you I hadn't done anything crazy in my entire life!'

'Then it was long overdue, don't you think?'

'My rebellion?' She snorted. 'Look where it got me.'

He shifted to sit beside her, perching on the edge of the sofa. 'We'll be all right, Tassy. Don't worry. Just give us time.'

He bent over and kissed her cheek, then without any fuss he put the rest of the fruit in the fridge, ran her a warm bath and took a glass of iced water up to her bedroom. When he came down he had her nightshirt and he put it in the bathroom and came out again, lounging against the doorpost and looking sexier than he had any right to look to her, given her fragile state of equilibrium.

'Can you manage, or do you want a hand?' he asked.

She got up and walked past him. 'I can manage. Thanks, Ben.'

She closed the bathroom door, leant back on it and stared blindly across the room as the tears leaked out of the corners of her eyes and dripped onto her soggy T-shirt. If only she was sure he loved her...

Sophie and Sam were both going home. Tassy, still struggling a little with nausea but learning now to deal with it a little better, spent time with both families, going through post-discharge care plans.

Sam's mother was looking forward to having him home after nearly ten weeks, but she was going to have to take time off to look after him unless her mother could come and stay. She was still trying to arrange it as she hadn't got enough money to take weeks off, and she was hopeful she could persuade her mother to come.

'Do impress on her the importance of his recovery, won't you?' Tassy said. 'He needs to continue with his rest and exercise programme—here are the details, but he knows what he has to do. Here are the details of his drugs, and what to look out for in side-effects. You do know he'll have to take penicillin for the rest of his life, don't you, to make sure he doesn't get a recurrence?'

'Yes, I do,' she nodded. 'Don't worry, we'll be careful.'

'And watch out for any of the symptoms coming back again. Pain, general feeling of illness, loss of appetite—don't think you'll suffer from that in a hurry, will you, Sam?' she said with a grin, and he giggled.

'Now, he knows how to take his pulse and what it should be, and he knows what jiggles are OK and what might not be, so if it gets faster, or jiggles in an unusual way, we need to know. Also if he gets breathless or pants. OK? I know it's a lot to remember but it's all written down. Here's the phone number of the clinic, and your appointment for a week's time to see how he's getting on, and you can always pop in and have a chat if you're unsure about anything—OK?'

Sam nodded, then prodded his mother.

'Oh—this is for you, and this is for Dr Lazaar. I don't suppose he's about so I can thank him?'

Tassy took the soft, flat package and Sam winked at her. 'It's gross,' he said in a stage whisper. 'I thought he could wear it for your wedding.'

Tassy blinked. She hadn't realised the children knew about their wedding, which was planned—by Mrs Lazaar—for ten days' time, the last Saturday in July. She still hadn't got a dress, and in fact had had very little to do with the plans. Ben had told her what was happening and tried to involve her, but she'd been listless and too nauseated to care.

On top of which, of course, she didn't really feel as if it was a proper wedding.

She thanked Sam and his mother for the presents, put them on one side and gave Sam a big hug, then waved them off. She didn't have time to look at the presents because Sophie's parents were there to take her home, and she had to go through the same procedure with them only with a different list of dos and don'ts.

'Don't let her walk about too much—a few minutes a day with crutches is ample. Lots of rest, watch out for swelling or discoloration of the toes, any increase in pain, a smell from the cast—anything which makes you think all is not well, and you must ring straight away. It's much better to phone and check than to assume it's not a problem. All right?'

Sophie nodded, and pulled something out from behind her back. 'This is for you,' she said, and beckoned Tassy closer. 'For the baby,' she whispered.

Tassy took the rather squiffy and somewhat grubby white kitten that Sophie had made, and swallowed the lump in her throat. 'Thank you, Sophie. How kind of you.'

'You might need to sew the head on a bit better—I had to rush it a bit.'

Tassy squashed the smile. 'I'm sure it will be fine. Thank you, sweetheart.'

She gave the child a hug, shook hands with the parents and watched them go, wondering how long it would be before they found something else to fight about. Maybe they'd got married for the wrong reasons, or without knowing each other well enough.

'Have I missed them?'

'Just. There's a present for you in my office from Sam.'

Ben nodded at the grubby bit of white fluff in her hands as they walked towards the office. 'What's that?'

'A present from Sophie—she made it for the baby.'

'Really? How sweet of her.'

'It's not safe, of course. I'll have to go over all the stitches again so bits don't come off which could get swallowed, but it was very kind of her. Here you are.' She passed him the little flat package and he looked at it suspiciously.

'Do you know what it is?'

She grinned. 'I have my suspicions.'

He opened the packet and removed a gaudy bit of silk. 'Good grief,' he said faintly.

Tassy laughed. It was Day-Glo green, with pink and orange hearts all over it, and it was without doubt the most ghastly tie she'd ever seen. 'He said it would be gross,' she told Ben when she could speak, and he shook his head in wonder.

'Have you seen this bit?' He held it up so she could study it, and sitting on the central pink heart were a pair of lovebirds, billing and cooing and batting their lashes.

'He said you could wear it for the wedding,' Tassy said, and Ben raised his eyebrows.

'Really?' he said doubtfully, eyeing the ghastly monstrosity with some suspicion. 'What did you get?'

She opened the present and took out a navy blue garter. '"Something blue", I imagine. How sweet of her.'

'Will you wear it?'

'Why not? I could do with a wedding dress, as well, I suppose.'

Ben chewed his lip. 'I've been thinking about that. I don't suppose you could wear that ball gown, could you, with the little jacket? It was stunning, and it's so elegant. You looked absolutely incredible in it. I can't imagine you looking better in anything, and I don't see you in yards of fluffy lace.'

Nor could Tassy, which was one reason why she hadn't been out shopping for a wedding dress yet. The other was cost—and it occurred to her suspicious mind that Ben might well be suggesting the ball dress on the grounds that it was bought. His parents seemed to be paying for everything else. Maybe he felt they'd done enough.

'I suppose I could wear it,' she said thoughtfully. 'I'll have another look at it tonight, then if it doesn't work I can get something tomorrow.'

It looked lovely, just as it had when she'd bought it, only now she was looking at it from a different perspective. Regardless, she thought she did like it and it would work. Whatever, it wasn't a proper wedding, she told herself, so it didn't matter.

Joan Lazaar was on the phone over the weekend, discussing last-minute arrangements. Tassy hoped she didn't think she was very ungrateful, but she just couldn't get excited about it. She felt tired and ill, and frankly would be glad when her pregnancy was over.

She saw Ben off early on Monday morning for a week-long course in Cambridge. He wouldn't be back till late on Friday and would go straight to his parents'. Josh was going to pick Tassy up on Saturday morning and take her to Norfolk for the wedding so she wouldn't

see Ben again until they were in the church where their
banns had been read the previous three Sundays.

There was a wedding in the church in the morning,
and so the flowers would all be arranged. There were to
be only a few close friends as guests. Josh and Melissa
Lancaster and Anna Long were the sum total of Tassy's
guest list. Ben's wasn't a great deal longer.

'What about your mother?' Ben had asked.

'What about my mother?' she'd replied, and nothing
more had been said.

She felt a pang of guilt over that, but she couldn't get
worked up about that either.

She got ready for work, sat down in the kitchen to eat
her breakfast and had a sudden, violent pain that stabbed
her low down in the abdomen. She gasped and dropped
her toast, and then as it eased she stood up and went
through to the sitting room and lay on the sofa. The pain
came and went for the next three hours, finally resolving
into a steady, nagging ache, and at some point in the
proceedings she rang the hospital and told them she
wouldn't be in.

She was losing the baby, she realised dimly, but she
couldn't work out what to do about it. Finally she rang
Anna, and she came over in her lunch-break and made
her up a bed on the sofa so Tassy didn't have to go up
and down stairs to the loo, which she was having to visit
with great frequency.

Anna also persuaded her to ring the GP, and he came
over during the afternoon and asked her lots of personal
questions, then assured her that she would probably be
fine. As it was at the time of her second period it was
likely that it would be not much more than a heavy period and she wouldn't need to go to hospital.

She wanted to talk to Ben, but he had exams and she didn't think it was fair. After all, there was nothing he could do so there was no point in worrying him. His mother had had her biopsy that day as well, she remembered, and wondered what the result had shown.

No, the last thing she could do was ring Ben up and tell him. She went to bed early with Sophie's kitten that she'd made for the baby and cried her eyes out, then took the next day off too, and on the Tuesday evening Ben rang her, shortly after Josh had. She'd fobbed him off with a story about a cold, but Ben was easier because he didn't know she'd been off work.

'How are you?' he asked, and she lied and said she was fine.

'Are you sure?' he asked, and she wondered for a second if Anna had said anything, but decided she couldn't have done or he would have been there. He was that sort of person and, anyway, she'd been sworn to secrecy. 'I'll tell Ben, but I don't want the others knowing yet,' she'd told her friend.

'I'm fine, truly,' she lied again to Ben. 'How's your mother? Any news?'

'No. I'll let you know if I hear. I miss you.'

Was it true, or just a line? She didn't want to know. Just then she needed it to be real.

'I miss you, too,' she told him truthfully. 'I wish you were here.'

'Don't worry, it'll soon be Saturday,' he assured her.

It was, altogether too soon. All the way there in the car with Josh and Melissa and Anna she was racked with guilt because she hadn't told Ben, but she hadn't really had a chance and she didn't feel it was something they could discuss over the phone. Anyway, once they were married there would be plenty of time—

No. She couldn't marry him without him knowing. They pulled up outside the little village church in the north Norfolk village at three minutes to three, just as Ben's parents were arriving.

Dr Lazaar came over and bent down and smiled at her through the car window. 'Hello, Tassy, dear. You look lovely. We're all ready for you.'

She swallowed. They might be ready, but she wasn't—not by a country mile. They got out of the car and Anna fussed over Tassy's jacket, arranged the flowers in her hair and made sure she'd got her bouquet the right way up. Then with a quick hug she disappeared inside the church with Melissa.

Josh offered her his arm, and she grabbed it like a lifeline and pulled him to a halt just inside the porch. 'Josh, I need to speak to Ben,' she told him urgently.

Josh searched her eyes, and then nodded. 'OK. Wait here, I'll get him.'

He slipped through the door, and she could hear the organist hesitate and then continue with the wallpaper music. She held her bouquet tightly, not sure how the words were going to come out or how any of it was going to come out.

'Tassy?'

She turned, took one look at him in Sam's awful tie and burst into tears. 'Tassy, darling, what is it?' he asked, folding her against his chest and rocking her.

'I need to speak to you,' she said through her tears.

'OK.' He put an arm round her shoulders and led her away from the church to a little seat under a yew tree. Then he sat down beside her and took her hand in his.

He was trembling, she noticed absently. Was he nervous about the wedding?

'What did you want to say, Tassy?' he prompted.

She swallowed, and took a deep breath. 'Ben, I lost the baby on Monday.'

He was silent for ages before very carefully, very gently, he pulled her into his arms and hugged her close. 'Oh, Tassy, I'm sorry.'

She let him hold her for a moment, then pulled away. 'I was going to just marry you without saying anything because I thought there would always be other times, other babies, but in the end I couldn't. I know you're only doing it because of your mother and, if you like, we can go ahead and just not tell her, and then at least she'll die thinking you were happy—'

'Tassy, Mum's not going to die. It was just a benign fatty cyst.'

Relief made her shoulders droop. 'Oh, Ben, I'm so glad for her—but that means we don't have to go through with this.'

He was silent for a long time, his fingers playing with hers, and when he spoke his voice was gruff and scrapy and he sounded as if he was holding himself together by a thread.

'Is that what you want?' he asked. 'Not to go through with it?'

Numbly, she shook her head. 'No. I want to marry you. I love you. I can't think of anything I want more in the world, but I don't want you feeling you have to go through with it under false pretences. I'll get over it, Ben, don't worry about me. Just do what you want.'

The tension drained out of him like air out of a punctured balloon. 'In that case,' he said with a wry smile, 'if you'd care to stop wrecking my nerves, perhaps we could go into the church and get this marriage under way—because I love you, Tassy Franklin, and I have ever since I met you, and if you imagine for one moment I'm letting you go now, at this stage, you've got another think coming.'

'Are you sure?' she asked doubtfully. 'What about your dream?'

'What about it? I was just using the baby as an excuse to marry you, but I'd actually like some time alone with you in the next couple of years to prove to you how much I love you. I'm sorry about the baby, of course, and I would love to have children one day, but don't imagine for a moment that that's why I wanted to marry you.'

'Oh,' she said weakly, and felt a foolish and enormous grin break out over her face.

'Oh, nothing. Come on. Everybody's waiting.'

She pulled him to a halt just outside the church, where Josh was hovering anxiously. 'Just one thing.'

His brows puckered together in a frown, betraying his still-jangled nerves. 'What?'

'Would you kiss me?'

He gave a short grunt of laughter, then pulled her into his arms. 'It would be my pleasure,' he said, and bent to capture her lips.

Josh cleared his throat and Ben released her, grinned at Josh and handed her back to him. 'Don't, for God's sake, let her sneak off,' he threatened, and went back into the church.

'Are you sure about this?' Josh asked her, and she laughed and nodded.

'Absolutely. I love him to bits, and he loves me, too. I'll explain later.'

'You'd better. You just took ten years off my life.'

The organist, cued at last, broke into the opening strains of 'Here Comes the Bride', and Tassy sailed down the aisle on Josh's arm, almost dragging him with her. At the end of the aisle she faltered.

'Mum?' she whispered.

'Hello, Tassy,' her mother whispered. 'You look beautiful, darling—quite beautiful.' She sniffed, and if Tassy hadn't known better she would have sworn those were tears in her eyes.

She looked at Ben in puzzlement and he winked at her. Releasing Josh's arm, she moved to stand beside the man she loved to make her vows.

She hardly heard the vicar's words. All she was conscious of was Ben beside her, his arm clamped round her and to hell with protocol, and when he slid the ring onto her finger her eyes filled with tears. After signing the register, he kissed her, just a gentle, modest, respectable kiss that smouldered with promise, and then, tapping her lightly on the nose with his finger, he turned her, took her arm and they walked down the aisle together. Everyone was smiling and looking relieved, as well they might after the scare she'd given them. None of them were more relieved than Tassy and Ben, she was sure of that.

'How did you get hold of my mother?' she asked him as they stood outside in the sunshine, waiting for the others to join them.

'I sneaked her number out of your address book. I thought she ought to be here.'

She turned to him. 'I thought you weren't sneaky and devious,' she said mildly.

He grinned. 'Only when necessary. Here's Mum. We'll tell her about the baby.'

'Won't it upset her?' Tassy said anxiously, not wanting to spoil Joan's day. 'We could tell her tomorrow.'

'No. She was panic-stricken when I came out. We need to tell her. Anyway, she'd rather think we married for love. Hi, Mum.'

'A moment of doubt?' Mrs Lazaar murmured to them.

'No, she had something to tell me. Mum, Tassy lost the baby on Monday.'

Her face creased with concern. 'Oh, darling, I'm sorry,' she said, taking Tassy's hands. 'Are you all right?'

She nodded and smiled. 'Better than all right. I know he married me because he loves me, and not because of the baby.'

'Well, of course he loves you! It's obvious.'

Tassy laughed. 'Not to me. I must be exceptionally dense.'

'Maybe,' Ben said with a grin.

'Definitely maybe,' Tassy replied with a smile, 'but I'm learning fast...'

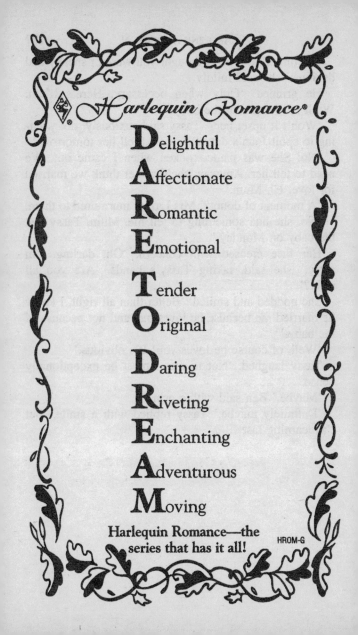

Harlequin Romance®

Delightful

Affectionate

Romantic

Emotional

Tender

Original

Daring

Riveting

Enchanting

Adventurous

Moving

Harlequin Romance—the
series that has it all!

HROM-G

HARLEQUIN  PRESENTS®

HARLEQUIN PRESENTS
men you won't be able to resist
falling in love with...

HARLEQUIN PRESENTS
women who have feelings
just like your own...

HARLEQUIN PRESENTS
powerful passion in
exotic international settings...

HARLEQUIN PRESENTS
intense, dramatic stories that will keep you
turning to the very last page...

HARLEQUIN PRESENTS
The world's bestselling romance series!

Harlequin® Historical

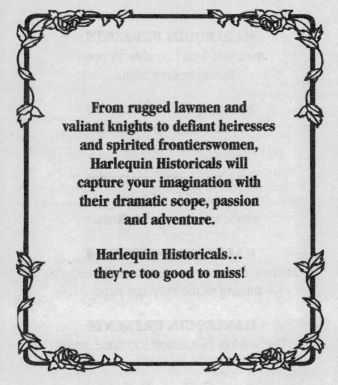

From rugged lawmen and
valiant knights to defiant heiresses
and spirited frontierswomen,
Harlequin Historicals will
capture your imagination with
their dramatic scope, passion
and adventure.

Harlequin Historicals...
they're too good to miss!

HHGENR

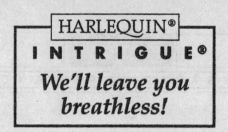

LOOK FOR OUR FOUR FABULOUS MEN!

Each month some of today's bestselling authors bring
four new fabulous men to Harlequin American Romance.
Whether they're rebel ranchers, millionaire power brokers
or sexy single dads, they're all gallant princes—and
they're all ready to sweep you into lighthearted fantasies
and contemporary fairy tales where anything is possible
and where all your dreams come true!

You don't even have to make a wish...
Harlequin American Romance will grant your every desire!

Look for Harlequin American Romance
wherever Harlequin books are sold!